GENERATIONAL CURSES

MY GRANDMOTHER'S SECRET

TAWANA N. WILSON, MSW

KishKnows
PUBLISHING

Generational Curses: My Grandmother's Secret
by Tawana N. Wilson, MSW

Cover design, editing, book layout, and publishing services by KishKnows, Inc., Richton Park, Illinois, 708-252-DOIT.
Cynthia C. Maloy, Main Editor

Dr. Kisia L. Coleman, Book Coaching & Consulting
admin@kishknows.com, www.kishknows.com

ISBN 978-0-578-28411-8

LCCN: 2022906218

Printed in the United States of America

TABLE OF CONTENTS

DEDICATION

Brenda...I could never have imagined that you wouldn't be here to help me celebrate the release of my first book. I miss you...I take solace in knowing that you are now with the Father. You fought and won. Rest well, Auntie. Love, Frizz.

Mum...You are the motivation and inspiration for this book. I could never forget you or the memories I've kept near and dear. You taught me so much, and your legacy lives on. Love, your number one grandchild.

Cynthia...To my dearest mommy and best friend. I love you more than I could ever put into words. I am so proud of you. You are a powerful Black woman, and I thank God for you daily. I will honor and cherish you for as long as I live. Love, your one and only daughter.

PROLOGUE

Essie could not believe her eyes as she watched what was happening in terror and utter disbelief. She had heard of things like this happening but had never experienced it. Not this close to home. She wanted to do something, but she was afraid. She wanted to say something, but she was frozen; not able to move and paralyzed with fear, hurt, devastation, and rage. She stooped behind the bushes so no one could see her. It seemed like forever had passed. Then it happened…She couldn't help what came out of her mouth next. "Andontis!" she yelled. Once they realized someone was watching, they turned a flashlight over to the area where Essie was hiding.

Essie saw the light and took off running. She was fast, and she knew they would never catch up with her, since she knew every crack and crevice of this place. Places that no one else knew about. She darted through bushes and down secret paths until she made it to the back door of her house.

Just as she opened the door, a car pulled up across the way, turning the headlights off so they would not be noticed. The men in the car watched the house but did not get out. They were not certain if the person who saw them was part of this family. They argued for a moment about whether they should go into the house and get the rest of them, then drove off.

Essie's mom got out of bed to see what was wrong with her. Essie was crying uncontrollably and could barely get a word out. She was hurt and afraid; but mostly, she was furious. After all, he was *good*. He was *respectful*. He got along with everyone. Why him? Finally, she had enough breath to say, "He's gone, Mama. They killed him." "Who?" her mother asked with a concerned look. "Who killed who, Essie? What are you talking about?"

1876 New Orleans, Louisiana
The Montgomery Plantation

Sarah, the eldest daughter of the Lavender family, cried and pleaded with Mister not to take him. Her oldest brother, Isaac, just sat there helpless, not saying anything because he was afraid; and he knew that if he spoke up, it would be him that they took instead. "Please don't do this! He's just a boy!" Mister punched Sarah so hard that she lost consciousness. Blood poured from her nose and mouth. Isaac still didn't move. Sarah's mother looked off in disgust, but she couldn't blame him. She knew it was hopeless. No one could save Samuel from what was about to happen. Grandma always knew the day would come—she just didn't know it would happen before Sammy was old enough to know what was going on. He was only eight years old.

When Sarah regained consciousness, she was in pain. Her grandmother was waiting with a rag soaked in aloe vera. She hopped up, searching around their cabin. When she realized her baby brother wasn't back yet, she became enraged. She went to her grandmother and said, "Show me." "Are you sure you want to do this?" Grandma asked. "There's no turning back if you open this door." Sarah nodded.

Grandma picked up a clay bowl that she had made from the very mud they rested on. She gathered some leaves and a lock of red hair from a large box that her grandfather had made from an oak tree that he had chopped down on the plantation. The hair belonged to Mr. Montgomery. Sarah had gotten it from his brush one time when they allowed her into the house to clean. As they worked, they heard a hard thump outside. It was Sammy, beaten and bruised. He had blood coming from his trousers where he'd just been violated by Mr. Montgomery and two of his friends. Grandma needed to make sure the person who did this would pay dearly. She wasn't confident that the hair was Mister's, so she had to further inflict pain on her grandson, but she promised him that it wouldn't happen again. She needed something that belonged to the person who assaulted her grandbaby. She laid Sammy across her lap that she had cushioned with a handmade blanket and pillow so he could at least be a little comfortable. After he settled, she took what was left of his trousers off and grabbed something that looked like a tree branch, then burned one end with the candle that they used to light their cabin. When the flame went out, she blew on it to cool it off, then asked Sarah to cover Sammy's mouth.

Grandma used the burned branch to collect what Mister and the others had left on Sammy. He didn't even scream…he was already hurt so badly that nothing else could possibly be any worse. Grandma began to chant. Once Sarah got used to the rhythm of the chant, she repeated it until they were chanting in unison. Then Grandma used the tree branch to collect the flesh of those vile owners from her grandson. She made sure she had what she needed before placing the branch in the clay bowl and set it on fire, still chanting.

A few days later, Sarah saw Mister being carried out on a stretcher. He had blood all over the front of his pants, and he was screaming in agony. No one knew what had happened. One of the housemaids told Grandma Lavender that Mister's bowels had exploded, and he was bleeding from his loins. His complications had only worsened during the time he had been in the hospital. The doctors had no idea how to help him, as they had never seen anything like it. His bowels had ruptured, and the waste had poisoned his blood stream. He was itching so badly that he scratched until it bled.

Nineteen days later, Mister died. When the Lavender family heard the news, they were overjoyed. They felt like he had finally gotten what he deserved. "He'll never touch any of us again!" one of them shouted. For some reason, their grandmother seemed troubled about his death. Sarah, her daughter and namesake asked, "Grandma, why don't you seem happy about this? What's the matter?"

Grandma said quietly, "He wasn't supposed to die." Then she stepped out of the cabin and cried until she couldn't cry anymore. Sarah didn't understand. Why was Grandma so upset? Wasn't this what they wanted to happen? There was talk about others who attended the barn party that night dying but nothing was ever confirmed. But there was never another party like that on the plantation again.

CHAPTER
ONE

IT was 10:17 pm, and Essie counted down the minutes, hoping to fall asleep before it began. Awakened out of a light doze, she glanced over at the clock…10:32 pm. "Miles, take your drunk self home to your wife." Essie heard the drunken slur with the Afro-American southern accent coming from outside her bedroom window and hopped up to see what the commotion was. It was Mrs. Addie Frank, her mama's good friend who came over at least twice a week to share the latest gossip. She was talking to a man that Essie only knew because of the yellow truck that he drove.

Their interaction was quite strange, Essie thought, as this man looked as if he owned Addie. Essie knew that Addie was married to Mr. Frank… in fact, everyone knew. She didn't understand what was going on. "Miles, I can't stand you." "C'mon, baby. Just this last time. I promise, you gon' love it." Addie's voice softened. "What am I gon' do with you, Miles?" Smiling, he whispered something in Addie's ear that made her laugh out loud and then she got into the yellow truck, and Essie heard it drive off.

Essie got back into bed and tried going back to sleep. The clock now read 11:40 pm, and she knew her mama would be coming in at 6:00 am to get her ready for school. Essie counted to herself, using her fingers and thinking, "If I get to sleep by midnight, I can get six whole hours of sleep." But she couldn't because the commotion coming from the Barnyard Tavern was as loud that night as it was any other night.

Sitting at her desk in her sixth-grade class, Essie said to herself, "I'm just gonna lay my head down on this desk for a second," even though she sat in the third desk from the front, right in front of the teacher. She thought to herself "My teacher ain't gon' care if I just laid my head here for a second." Essie heard her teacher call her name, but she couldn't move because she was so tired. "Essie," she heard again but louder this time. She still didn't move...she was so tired, falling deeper and deeper to sleep. "ESTER RENAE LAVENDER, GET YO TAIL UP!" Startled, she jerked awake and looked up to see her mother standing there with her arms folded and a scowl on her face. The clock read 6:07 am.

Once her mother knew that Essie was fully awake, she told her to go and wash up so that her sister could get in after her. Essie got her panties, undershirt, and socks from the small table where her mother laid her things out every night, went into the bathroom and turned on the sink then stood there, looking at herself in the mirror for a second. Some days, she stared off, daydreaming; other days, she looked at herself and wondered why she looked the way she did.

Essie was the fourth of her parents' five children. She had an older brother, two older sisters, and a younger brother. Andon Jr., the oldest, was nineteen years old. He was her protector and looked out for her. He no longer stayed in the house, but he visited often. Sara was seventeen and named after her great-grandmother...a family tradition. Every firstborn daughter was named Sarah...and she looked exactly like her mother. She was still in the house but stayed out of sight as often as she could, because she hated it so much. She often talked about how she couldn't wait to leave their town. Naomi was sixteen...she was the "good" girl. She loved school and got good grades. She was very respectful and helped around the house. Naomi worked odd jobs and always gave the money to her mom or bought gifts for Essie and their younger brother who had just turned seven years old. They had a small two-bedroom house with an attic. The attic had been Andon Jr.'s room before he moved out and now Sara spent most of her time there. Essie and Naomi shared a room, and the baby boy still slept in the room with their mom when their dad wasn't home. He slept in Essie and Naomi's room when their father was home.

Dad worked at the Mill like a lot of the Black men in town. Mama was a maid for the Montgomery family. The Montgomery and Lavender families had ties that went back many generations. Essie's great-grandmother and grandmother were born on the Montgomery plantation. By the time her grandmother Sarah Mae was thirteen, the slaves had been emancipated, and slavery had ended (in name, anyway), but she decided not to leave with the rest of her family who lived and worked there.

About sixty-five years earlier...

"Sarah Mae, let me talk to you for a second." Sarah had known that this conversation would happen, so she wasn't surprised when Mr. Montgomery asked to speak to her privately. "I've watched you grow into a decent young lady, and I would hate for you to get out there in the world and not survive. It's a cold, cold world out there, and other Negroes would love to take advantage of a girl like you. My wife and I would like to offer you room and board for as long as you want. But we'd like for you to continue working for us. You won't have to worry about meals…they will be provided by us. You will have a comfortable room where you can come and go as you please. You will have specific work hours, and we will pay you outside of what we charge you for room and board." "How much y'all gon' pay?" Sarah asked. "We will work something out. Don't worry because every week, you will get paid." Sarah was not totally confident about this deal, but she knew why he wanted her to stay. Sarah wanted to stay too but for a different reason. One that would haunt her bloodline for centuries to come. "Okay," she said with a seductive look. His eyes followed her. "Lock the door." Sarah Mae got up and did what she was told.

Essie lay in the bed, wide awake at 11:40 pm. She remembered falling asleep well before the Barnyard had opened, but loud drunken arguing had awakened her. After looking at the clock, she looked over at Naomi who always seemed to sleep through the loud ruckus and wondered to herself how on earth could she sleep through this.

Essie looked out her window. She didn't see anything, but she heard it all. She got out of her bed and tiptoed through the house, being careful not to disturb anything. It was very quiet except when she got to her parents' room where her father's snoring sounded like a truck was coming from his mouth. Essie walked back to her bedroom and sat up in her bed. The clock read 12:16 am; she began to count, then stopped because she was not in the mood to sleep.

Essie grabbed her sweater and shoes and tiptoed out the back door, leaving it unlocked so she could let herself back in. She knew she couldn't let anyone see her because everyone knew her and her family. The town was small, and she would be in trouble if she got caught.

The Barn was situated at the corner of the block, two houses down from the Lavender residence. The house in between was vacant, and many of the Barn-goers would hang around that house too. Essie did not want to take the main road, so she walked the back road, ducking behind garbage cans, and hiding in the bushes when she thought someone noticed her. This excited Essie for some reason. Her adrenaline was high, and the rush made her feel good. She finally made it to the Barn… and then thought to herself, "Now what?"

The Barn was a beat-up shack where the town folks would go to unwind and enjoy themselves after a long day. It never closed; and after 10:00 pm, it would get loud, and the noise would last into the wee hours of the morning. Sometimes, people would party all night, then go straight to work the next morning. There was a window in the front of the barn where anyone could look in and see what was going on. There was a boarded-up window upstairs and two more boarded up windows in the back on each side of the exit. There was also a hidden window in the back that few paid attention to.

The Barn had two floors: the main floor and the attic. The hidden window was at the back, at the bottom of the stairs. Essie went down the stairs, where the stench of urine, liquor, and cigars was overwhelming.

She covered her nose and mouth with the sleeve of her sweater and peeked in the window, where she could only see the feet of the people at the bar and a few of the Barn-goers who were dancing, while others stood near the front windows or by the jukebox. Essie positioned herself so she could connect the shoes with the person. It wasn't overly exciting, but it was interesting enough to keep her eyes glued to the window until she felt herself getting sleepy again.

"Get up, Essie!" She heard her mama on the first try. When she opened her eyes, her mama smiled and said, "Good morning, Baby Cakes,"—her childhood nickname. Essie grabbed her clothes from the table and went to the bathroom to wash. Standing in front of the mirror, she noticed that the whites of her eyes were slightly reddened, and the bags underneath looked a bit heavier than usual. Essie and her siblings had the most beautiful blue eyes, inherited from their grandfather, the one that they had never met or even talked about. Her mom was beautiful, with long, flowing black hair, fair skin, and blue eyes. Naomi and Sarah looked almost identical to their mom, except Naomi did not have the same eyes that the rest of them had. Her eyes were hazel and could look green or gray depending on the light. Andon Jr. looked almost identical to their dad.

CHAPTER
TWO

SPRING quickly turned to summer, and Essie made sneaking out to the Barnyard Tavern a ritual when she couldn't sleep, which was often. She enjoyed sneaking out and spying on folks, learning all the secrets and scandals that were taking place in town. Essie knew the people…even if they didn't know her.

One night, she was down at her regular spot a little after midnight. She heard a familiar voice but ignored it because she knew her brother wasn't home. She went back to her people-watching, then she felt some-one grab her arm so hard that she cried out in pain. "What the hell are you doing here, Essie?" Andon Jr. was looking at her with concern. "Where's Ma? Is she okay?" Andon had a friend with him. She had seen the guy a few times but didn't know much about him. She didn't think that he was a regular at the Barn.

Andon practically dragged Essie home; but before they got to the door, she pleaded with him not to tell on her. He had a soft spot for Essie, so he made her promise to never sneak out again. He told her to turn out the porch light when she got inside so that he knew she was safe. Essie peeked out the window before going to her room. She watched as the guy that Andon was with attempted to grab his hand. She thought it was weird, because it wasn't normal for a man to grab another man's hand in that way. Andon looked up and noticed Essie in the window, then yanked his hand away.

Later that morning, Essie was awakened by loud chatter and cackles from her mom, Mrs. Addie Frank, and another lady from town gossiping while having coffee. Essie went down to the kitchen. She spoke to the ladies, hugged her mother, and went to the fridge. She heard Mrs. Addie Frank whisper something and said, "Are you talking about Miles?" Her mom spit her coffee out, and Mrs. Addie Frank looked as if she'd seen a ghost. Her mom asked, "What did you say, Essie?" Mrs. Addie Frank and the other lady looked at each other in shock, and Mrs. Addie Frank said angrily, "This is why I don't talk about grown folks' stuff in front of kids, 'cause they too grown and too nosey, always in grown folks' business." Essie's mother said indignantly, "Well, I don't talk about grown folk stuff in front of my kids if that's what you trying to say." "I ain't tryna say nothing," Addie said, pointing in Essie's direction. Essie just looked at Mrs. Addie Frank and smirked.

The other woman felt how intense the situation was becoming so she gathered her things, thanked Essie's mom for the coffee and hospitality, and asked Mrs. Addie Frank to walk with her. They left, and her mother was so offended at Mrs. Addie Frank's accusation that she totally forgot to talk to Essie about what she said.

It was a hot summer Saturday, and everyone was home except Dad, who never took a day off. Sara was upstairs in the attic, as usual. The baby boy was sitting on the back steps with a friend, and Naomi was still in the bedroom asleep. Essie fixed herself a bowl of cereal and went to watch cartoons. She must have fallen asleep because she woke up and heard her mom ask Naomi, "Are you okay? "Get up and get started on your chores. Why are you sleeping so late?" "I don't know. I'm just tired, Ma," Naomi said.

Essie got up and took her bowl to the sink, then went to the bedroom. The door was slightly closed so she peeked in to make sure Naomi wasn't getting dressed. She saw Naomi pull something out from under the bed wrapped in what looked like a knitted blanket. Essie couldn't tell what it was, but Naomi took the cap off and took a swallow, then wrapped it back up, put it back in the box, and pushed it back under the bed. After Naomi put on her house shoes, Essie entered the room. "Hey, Essie Renae," Naomi said enthusiastically, "Give me a hug." Essie hugged her big sister back and said, "Hey, Nawni. You smell like medicine," "I know. I just took a little sip of cough syrup. I haven't been feeling too good lately."

Later that evening...

Essie couldn't wait until everyone went to bed so she could go to the Barn. It was summer so the days were longer, and school was out so the house stayed lit longer than usual. Finally, Naomi went to bed. Essie waited for about an hour after she'd gone to sleep before she stepped out. She got to her normal spot; and just as she got settled, she saw Miles come out of the back door with a strange lady.

Miles and his lady were kissing and hugging on each other, and he was whispering in her ear. He couldn't keep his hands off her, and she looked like she was enjoying it. Miles ran his fingers through her hair and over her face, then rubbed his hand across her lips. Essie was confused and thought the lady had to be gross for letting him put his nasty hands in her mouth without washing them. Miles guided the woman, hugging her from behind while practically pushing her in the direction of his truck. They got into his yellow pick-up truck, but he didn't drive off.

Essie turned her attention back to the Barn. A few minutes later, she heard the yellow truck screech off; and when she turned her head, she found herself looking right into the eyes of the woman who had gotten into the truck with Mr. Miles...and to her surprise, it was the woman who had coffee with her mama and Mrs. Addie Frank that morning! The woman looked at Essie for what seemed like an eternity, then turned her head, walked past the Barnyard, and went on her way.

The next day…

"I saw your mama at the Barn last night," said Essie to one of the girls she was riding the merry go round with. They both laughed as if Essie were joking. "I'm for real," she said. "She had on that little polka dot dress that she loves so much. You know the one…she wears it to church, to the grocery store, to do laundry…you know her favorite dress?" Essie said with a grin. One of the girls was still laughing but the other was obviously mad that Essie would treat her this way; after all, they were friends. "You're lying. How you see my mama at the Barnyard? Kids can't even go to the Barn, and my mama don't even like that place because she said it's too noisy and ain't no earthly bit of good in that place, so stop lying!" Essie said, "I ain't lying…why I gotta lie for?"

The girl got in Essie's face and balled up her fists. "Well, my mama said your house is full of demons, 'cause your grandma was a whore and a voodoo witch who slept with White men for money, and she cursed y'all whole family! I believe it too, 'cause y'all eyes blue, and they change colors. Black people don't got eyes like that. My mama told me not to play with you 'cause your mama and grandmamma are witches!" She stormed off as the tears began to flow. Essie was furious at what her friend's mom had said about her family. She wondered why her friend would say such nasty things, forgetting that she had started it when she told her about her mom and the Barn.

Essie had grown confident in her visits to the Barnyard every night. She felt a sense of empowerment. Whenever she saw someone from town and knew their scandals or secrets, that devilish grin became the "I know what you did" stare, as if she was the only one who knew what it meant.

Essie couldn't wait to see what secrets would unfold tonight at the Barnyard. She decided to turn in early…or pretend to at least. It was only 7:00 pm, but Essie figured that if she went to bed, then everyone else would too. However, it was summertime, and everyone was still out. Mama had worked late at the Montgomery's, Daddy had been gone since Friday, and Sara was in the attic. She had to look after Essie and the baby boy while Mom and Dad worked. Naomi was still out somewhere, and Essie wondered where she was because she couldn't go to the Barnyard unless Naomi was in bed sleeping.

Essie woke up the next morning to the sound of arguing. "I want to make my own money and pay my way out of here!" Sara yelled. "You need to find another way, Sara. I'm sorry. You're so much better than this." "I knew it," Sara cried. "You want me to remain stuck here like you and all the other folks in this town. Every time I get the opportunity to work toward something, you interfere. I hate it here!"

By this time, Essie was standing in the doorway of her bedroom. She was fuming because it was morning, and she had slept through the entire night and missed her nightly outing to the Barnyard. As Sara stomped up to the attic, Essie slammed her bedroom door as hard as she could, startling her mama and stopping Sara in her tracks. They looked at one another puzzled, then her mother walked over to the room and opened the door. "What's the matter, Baby Cakes?" Essie had to think of something quickly, because she didn't want her mama knowing the real reason she was so upset. "I hate it when y'all argue like this." Essie saw how this moved her mother, so she squeezed some tears from her eyes to make it a bit more theatrical.

Once Mama saw how distraught Essie was, she embraced her and said, "I'm sorry, Baby Cakes. I only want what's best for my children. I want you all to be better…to live better than me. I will die before I allow y'all to go through any of that mess, and I mean it." Her mother's voice quivered as she spoke. She wiped Essie's tears asking, "You okay now, baby?" Essie nodded her head, and Mama went upstairs to talk to Sara. Once her mama was out of hearing range, Essie buried her head in her pillow, laughing at the show she had just put on.

"Can I come in?" Mama knocked on the attic door, then hearing nothing, she let herself in. Sara was sitting in the window on the other side of the room, facing the backyard. The window was a huge oval with enough space for two people to sit comfortably. This was her regular spot, where she often sat and daydreamed about leaving and making a life separate from her family.

"Sara, I just want you to understand why I'm against this." Sara stared at her. "How can you be against it when you've worked for them your entire life?" "That's exactly why," Mama said. "I know them; and even though I've worked with them, I would never want you to work there." Sara started to cry again and asked Mama why, but she just put her head in her hands and said, "Baby, one day you will understand, but now is not the time."

THREE

ESSIE was in her room, trying to figure out how she could have slept through the Barn noise the night before. She felt anxious about missing out. She looked over at Naomi's bed and thought, "Where is she?" Then she remembered the cough syrup that Naomi took that day and the box that she had pushed under the bed. She decided to look and see what was in that box. The box was so far under the bed that Essie had to stretch to reach it. The box was heavy, but she managed to maneuver it out from under the bed. It was wooden, with a rusted latch that had no lock.

Essie flipped the latch over. The box had a bunch of stuff in it—maxi pads, pens, notepads, a bottle of perfume, a few pieces of jewelry, a man's watch, and Naomi's diary. Essie pulled that out and put it to the side. The cough syrup was wrapped and was so far buried in the box that Essie practically had to empty the entire thing to get to it. Finally, she got the bottle unwrapped and read "Canadian Reserve Whiskey" on the front. Essie was no dummy…she knew exactly what it was. She couldn't believe that it was Naomi's though. Naomi was good!

"Wow! Nawni drinks?" Essie thought. "I never see her at the Barn!" She wrapped up the bottle and put everything back in the box like she found it, so that Naomi wouldn't know she had gone through her things. She put everything back except for the diary. She picked it up and closed the bedroom door, then got into bed and crawled under the covers. Making herself comfortable, she opened Naomi's diary and opened it to an entry that read Saturday, May 15th.

The people in this house just ignore me. No one knows or cares what happened to me. I wish I could tell my mom or Daddy, but they probably wouldn't believe me. I hate myself. I want to disappear. How could God let this happen to me? I am such a fool. How could I be this naïve. No one can know.

After reading this, Essie began hunting through Naomi's diary in search of what had happened. She went through the pages frantically but became frustrated when nothing told her what she wanted to know. Then she heard a loud crash outside the door and her mom yelled, "What on Earth?" Essie opened the door to see Naomi laid out on the floor. From the look of things, she had tried to sit down and missed the chair. She was sitting there, examining her elbow because she hit it on the floor on her way down. Sara stood at the top of the stairs that led the attic, staring at her sisters and her mother in disgust before shaking her head and going back to her room.

Mama rushed over to Naomi to help her up. "Baby, are you okay?" she asked, while helping Naomi to her feet. "I'm fantastic, Mommy," Naomi said with a slur. "Oh my God! Are you drunk?" "Calm down, Ms. Lavender. It ain't a travesty. What's been going on here? Did you miss me?" She tried to hug Sarah, but she stopped her and said, "You stink. Where have you been?" "Funny you should ask that now, given that I've been gone all night. Did you even notice? I could have been dead in a ditch somewhere for all you care!" Sarah just stood there in denial. She couldn't believe that this was Naomi. Naomi stumbled to the bedroom, and Essie quickly hid the diary under her mattress. Naomi laid across her bed and fell into a deep, drunken sleep, but Essie waited until the coast was clear to continue reading. Her mom came into the bedroom a few minutes later, carrying a mug of something, aspirin, and a towel with ice on a tray. She set the tray down on the same table where she put Essie's clothes for school, then sat down on the bed where Naomi was sleeping. She pulled her up without saying a word and cradled her like she did when she was a baby. She put the aspirin in Naomi's mouth, and then she put the mug to her lips… "Here, baby. Just take a swallow."

After Naomi took a few swallows, she laid back against her mother. Sarah then placed the ice pack on Naomi's elbow, positioning herself so that she could get comfortable in her arms and began to hum a familiar melody. Essie studied her mother. She had heard her mother humming the tune often, usually while cleaning the house or washing the dishes.

Mama continued to hum and cradle Naomi, then began to sob loudly. Her grip on Naomi tightened as she yelled out, "You cannot have my children! I change my mind! I cancel all your plans against my family right now. You cannot have my children! Loose them right now! You have no power in this household. I decree and declare this household blessed. You are defeated, demon, and I cast you down to the pits of hell where you belong. My God is my strong tower, and He shows himself mightily through my Lord and Savior Jesus Christ. I look to the hills from which my help comes, and my help comes from the Lord! Praise the Name above all Names, Jesus Christ. Have your way in this place, Jesus! Have thine own way. Break those generational strongholds, Lord!" Still sobbing, she began to speak in the spiritual tongue. Then Naomi began to weep. "I'm so sorry," she said over and over. Mama continued to rock back and forth, still speaking in tongues. Essie heard the baby boy in the kitchen and left the room to tend to him while Mama got Naomi together.

The house was unusually peaceful for the rest of the day. Around 6:30 pm, Sarah was in the kitchen preparing dinner, and Naomi was still resting in the bedroom. The baby boy played in the backyard not too far from the back door. Mama kept a close eye, checking on him every few minutes. Essie came in and greeted her mom. "Hey, Baby Cakes. Go get washed up for dinner."

A few minutes later, Essie came back into the kitchen and her face lit up when she saw Andon Jr. sitting at the dinner table playing with the baby boy. "Hey A.D.," Essie said as her big brother picked her up and hugged her, then kissed her cheek. "Hey, Baby Girl, how are you doing?"

"Fine," Essie said. Sarah began preparing plates and setting them on the table. Essie looked at her strangely as she set a plate for Daddy, Naomi, and Sara, when none of them were there. It was very rare that the family would have dinner together at the table.

Mama prepared her plate, then sat down with a peaceful and delighted look on her face, which further confused Essie. Then her dad came through the back door. Essie was so happy to see him. He gave Sarah a kiss, shook A.D.'s hand, kissed Essie on the head, then went to wash his hands for dinner. Sara joined them at the table and then Naomi came in. Essie was the only one at the table who looked disturbed. Everyone else was talking and acting like a normal family, but Essie wondered what was going on. She liked that her family was together, but she also wondered how long they were going to keep up with the charade. She also wondered if she would be able to get to the Barnyard tonight.

The clock in Essie's and Naomi's bedroom said 12:52 am. Naomi was asleep, A.D. had left after dinner, and Sara and the baby boy were asleep in the attic. However, it sounded like a party in her parents' room. The radio was playing, and Essie could smell the liquor her daddy had brought for them. She was so mad she could cry. Then she heard her parents' bed creaking and lit up, because she knew she would be able to get to the Barnyard after all.

At 1:15 am, Essie made her way past her parents' room. She knew it was safe because her dad was snoring—the sign that the coast was clear whenever he was home. By this time of night, most of the folks in the Barn were half past drunk. Essie was sleepy, but she was determined not to miss tonight, so she forced herself to stay awake.

Essie showed up later than usual. As she started to walk down the back steps to her normal spot, she stopped and did a double take. She noticed the guy that had been with A.D. the night he caught her at the Barnyard. Then she noticed A.D. She could not believe her eyes as she zeroed in and continued to watch what was going on. She heard her brother cry out in pain. This startled her so she ran, then stopped, because she thought if something was happening to Andon, she could witness it and tell someone. When she looked down the steps again, she saw that the guy was facing A.D. and they were hugging and kissing in ways that a woman and man would. "Why can't we have this?" "C'mon man. I told you already. We would be killed if anyone found out about this," Andon said. "It's bad enough that us niggas ain't good enough around here. Just imagine the kind of life we would have. You know we can't."

A.D. looked disgusted with the guy and pushed him away. "I want a wife and kids someday. This ain't no permanent thing with me, Ray, and I done told you that before. Just stop it, 'cause it ain't gon' ever happen. Ever!" "I love you, and I don't care what people say or think. That's the sacrifice I am willing to make for us...for our love," Ray said while moving closer to A.D. "I don't love you, Ray."

This broke Ray's heart. A.D. started to walk up the steps, and Essie took off running, making it back to her bed just as her father peeked in to check on them like he did whenever he was home. Confused and disappointed at what she just discovered about her big brother; Essie cried herself to sleep. She didn't cry because of what her brother was doing, but because of what would happen to him if anyone found out.

One week later

Essie decided to walk the main road to the Barn. There was something strange about this night. She had an eerie feeling; and as she got closer to the Barn, her heart started to race. That wasn't enough for her to turn around and go back home because she didn't want to miss anything, so she kept walking down the main road. The street was darker than normal, and people looked like zombies. Everything was in slow motion, and the Barn seemed farther away than usual. As Essie got closer, she felt an excruciating pain in her stomach. She placed both hands over the pain and kept walking. Once she made it, she noticed the regular folks were all at her hiding spot, looking, pointing, and laughing. As she pushed through the crowd to see what happened, she saw A.D. and Ray again. A.D. was behind Ray…but when Ray turned around, it was her daddy's face. This startled Essie, and she turned to run away but her friend was standing there, laughing at her…the one that Essie had taunted about her mother's polka dot dress. She stood there and wouldn't let her pass. Essie felt the pain in her stomach worsen. She looked down and realized that her friend had stabbed her, and there was blood pouring from her stomach.

Essie woke up screaming and looking at her bloodied hands. Naomi woke up and rushed to her bed. While she was trying to wake Essie, she kept saying "I'm not going no more! I won't go no more!" "Essie, wake up!" Naomi yelled. "It's just a dream—Essie, wake up!"

Once Essie realized that it was just a dream, she was relieved to see Naomi and cried hard in her arms. Naomi comforted her baby sister saying, "It's okay. Shh… It's okay, Essie. It was just a dream." Essie still felt the pain in her stomach. She told Naomi that she had had a dream that her friend stabbed her in the stomach and that she was bleeding. Naomi got up and went to the kitchen. She came back with the tray that her mother had used when she hit her elbow. Naomi turned on the light, and there was blood on Essie's bedsheets and blanket. She said, "Oh, Essie! You got your period!"

Naomi taught Essie everything she needed to know about that time of the month. She explained that every month, she should have her period. She told Essie that it was important to keep up with the date of her period for two reasons: 1. You could have an accident. 2. If you don't get your period then you're pregnant, and you don't want that either. Not right now, at least. "Most of the time, you'll have cramps the first few days and maybe a day or two before it actually comes." "Cramps?" Essie asked. "Yes, cramps. That's the pain you feel in your stomach right now. Sometimes, you won't have cramps though, and your period could sneak up on you. Never take a bath while you're on your period." Essie frowned and looked perplexed. Naomi noticed Essie's facial expression and got lost in her thoughts. Looking at her baby sister and how innocent she was made her flashback to the time when her innocence was taken away. "I know that sounds crazy, Es. If you take a bath in the tub, then you'll be on your period longer. You are supposed to wash up or use this." She held up a reddish-orange rubber bag with a long string and what looked like the opening of a water hose on the end. Essie burst out laughing and said, "Now, how am I supposed to wash up with that?" Naomi looked at what she was holding, and they both laughed so hard that they totally forgot about what was troubling them.

CHAPTER
FOUR

THE start of the new schoolyear was just a week away. Sara was taking classes at the community college, working at the grocery store three nights a week and at the laundromat on the weekends. She was almost never home but that was how she preferred it. Her home and family were a constant reminder of everything she didn't want to be.

Sara had a good friend named Ashlynn. Ashlynn was part heir to the Montgomery plantation where her mom worked. The two met on the plantation when they were children and became good friends. Unlike the rest of the Montgomery clan, Ashlynn valued people—all people—regardless of their skin color. They both knew that the friendship would be forbidden outside of the plantation, but they talked as much as they could. Devlynn Montgomery was the sole heir to the Montgomery Plantation and Ashlynn's great-grandmother. She absolutely hated "nigras," which was what she called all Black people. But Mrs. Devlynn carried a few secrets herself, just like her father and grandfather. They openly hated Black people but also secretly admired them. Mrs. Devlynn often watched Sarah while she cooked and cleaned, how she was with the Montgomery children, and even watched how good she was with her own children. She would never tell Sarah that she admired her...in fact, she made it her mission to let her know that she was better than Sarah in all her ways. Sarah was much smarter than Mrs. Devlynn though, and she often dumbed down a bit to appease her. She had learned everything she knew from her grandmothers, who had all worked on the plantation. Sarah's mother, whose name was also Sarah, was born there, grew up there, got to know the Montgomerys well, and had even decided to stay there and work even after she was allowed to leave and live on her own.

"Grandmother, their family has worked here for years. I think she'd be a great maid here. She could work with her mother or on the days her mother doesn't work." "Of course she would, darling. I just don't know if it's a good idea." "Why wouldn't it be?" "Darling, befriending a nigra is not good for the Montgomery's reputation. I know you mean well but her being here too much just isn't good." Mrs. Devlynn would never tell her the real reason she didn't want Sara to work in their home. "Grandmother, you're not being fair. She is my friend. She needs a job, and you know you could help her!" Ashlynn looked at her grandmother for a minute, then said, "Okay," and started to walk out the office. "I'll think about it," Mrs. Devlynn said before Ashlynn got to the door. "Thanks, Grandmother," Ashlynn said. Although their plans to have Sara work on the plantation failed, Sara secured two jobs at companies that were owned and run by the Montgomery family.

Essie was going into the eighth grade, and Naomi was a senior in high school. The baby boy was going into the second grade and stayed with Mrs. Addie Frank after school until Sarah got off work, or Naomi picked him up. Andon Jr. left New Orleans to join the Navy.

Three years later

Essie was sixteen and a junior in high school. Her quests to the Barnyard continued. She had really grown over the past three years. She was gorgeous but she always had been. Her entire family was good looking. Their father was quite handsome. He was at least six feet tall and darker than them all. His dark complexion and their mother's lighter complexion set the tone for Essie and the baby boy. The rest of the children were shades of high yellow except Andon Jr., who was the darkest of them all.

Essie had a good group of friends; a few of them went to the same high school and lived in the neighborhood, and their families knew one another well. Others attended the same high school but lived in different neighborhoods. One of Essie's closest friends, Jeanie, lived on the west side of town in the Shallow Point Housing Projects in the Fischer Dev Neighborhood. Although they attended the same high school, the first time they crossed paths was at the Barnyard Tavern one night.

Jeanie had wandered way over that way, looking for her sister who had recently begun working at the Barn as a barmaid. Some stuff had happened at home, and she desperately needed to find her. For some reason, Jeanie decided to take the back road once the Barnyard was in sight. She had never been there or even been to that part of town. Her sister had told her about the job and where it was but had made her promise not to tell anyone. A few feet away from the back exit of the Barn, Jeanie noticed a guy taking a pee by some bushes and hurried past. "Hey, cutie! Where are you going?" He skipped ahead so he could catch up with her then grabbed her wrist. "Hey, hey, hey. Slow down Li'l Mama. What's the rush?" Jeanie looked confused as she tried to unlock her wrist from his grip. The guy pulled her closer and began to back her into a dark corner. "Let me go!" she yelled. "Why?" The guy said as he groped her and leaned in to try and kiss her. She started to cry and begged him to please stop…Essie was in her spot again when she heard a voice. She went to investigate and noticed James Bevineau harassing a young woman who looked terrified. "What are you doing, James?" By now James had a good grip on Jeanie, and she was totally helpless. He looked back but didn't loosen his grip. "Mind your business," he said. Essie moved closer. "This is my business," she said, folding her arms. James was annoyed and was about to go off until he noticed it was Essie. "Essie, what are you doing around here? I know your mama don't know you out here this late?" "I'm out here making sure girls aren't getting raped," Essie scowled. James was taken aback by this and tried to play it off. "Raped?" He asked like he was offended. "Essie, you are young, but you know better than that. This is my girl." Essie wasn't convinced.

James was very handsome. He had most of the girls in town, and the ladies loved him. Even Naomi had dated him for a while. Jeanie looked at Essie and shook her head. "Do you know him?" Essie said. "No. I was looking for my sister," Jeanie replied. Essie felt sorry for her. She had to think of something and fast. James was much stronger than they were, so she said, "So are you out here raping people now, James?" She said it as loud as she could to draw attention their way and put the emphasis on *raping*. James looked at her like she had lost her mind, but she kept at it. "I wonder what your daddy would think if he found out his son James was a raper man. "Police, James the raper man is over here," Essie hollered. People standing around the Barn looked their way and started walking toward them. She wouldn't stop with the insults, so James backed away and ran off.

"Thank you," Jeanie said as she fixed her clothes. "Are you okay?" Essie asked. "Not really." Jeanie looked at Essie like she was crazy for even asking. They found a little humor in this plight. "You said you were looking for your sister? Who is she? What's her name?" "Her name is Jennifer, and she works here," said Jeanie. Essie said, "Oh! The new waitress? I can show you where she is, but I can't take you in there."

Essie took Jeanie down to her spot and peeked through the window. She spotted the new barmaid and pointed her out, then showed Jeanie where to go and disappeared. When Jeanie doubled back to ask Essie's name and to thank her again, she was gone.

On the way home, Essie thought about Jeanie and wondered what could have happened to make her travel to the bar alone, in the middle of the night.

CHAPTER
FIVE

A few days had passed since Essie and Jeanie crossed paths. Essie was in her English class finishing up the assignment when the bell rang. She usually met a few of her friends in the hallway to walk to their next class together.

Essie needed to stop at the restroom before heading to class, and the other two girls decided to keep walking. "If he takes attendance before I get there, let him know I'm on my way."

Essie was in the stall when she heard a familiar voice but couldn't place it. When she came out, she went to the sink to wash her hands and saw Jeanie standing there with a few other girls. "Jeanie? Hey!" Essie embraced her like she had known her for a long time. Jeanie appeared rattled and looked at Essie like she didn't know her. "Hey," Jeanie said hesitantly. Essie was not paying attention to Jeanie's behavior. "What grade are you in?" "I'm a Freshy," she said. The girls that Jeanie was with scowled at Essie, and one of them said, "Come on Jeanie, 'fo' we be late…" Jeanie turned around when she got to the door and said, "Bye." "See you," Essie replied.

On the walk to the bus stop, Essie and her girlfriends chatted, talking about school and repeating the latest gossip. "Remember when I told y'all about the new waitress at the Barn and her sister?" The girls nodded. "She goes to Bremar!" Essie said excitedly. "Why you all frantic?" one of them said. "I don't know," she said, shrugging her shoulders,

"I was just wondering what had happened to her."

Later that evening, Essie was in her usual spot at the Barn. After running into Jeanie, she was interested in knowing more about her sister, Jennifer. Peeking through the window, she watched Jennifer closely. "She's pretty," Essie thought, and noticed that she and Jeanie looked alike. They both had small waists with Coke bottle shapes. They both had dark skin tones, but they were pretty. (Not only did White people think Black people with dark skin were ugly and unattractive, but some Black people also considered dark skin to be ugly and unattractive.) Jennifer had long, flowing hair that didn't look like it belonged to her. Jeanie always wore two French braids, one on each side of her head. Watching Jennifer was boring because she added no excitement to the Barn. She took orders, smiled at the partygoers, and kept to herself. She was a new face, so everyone wanted a piece of her, but she wasn't interested in any of them. She did her job and went home.

Essie watched her for a couple of days until she knew her routine; then one night, she waited until Jennifer's shift ended just to see the route she took home. To Essie's surprise, Jennifer drove a car to and from the Barn. It was nothing fancy; just an old, beat-up hatchback.

"Hey, Jeanie," Essie said as she and her friends passed her in the hallway. Jeanie glanced at Essie and waved. One of the girls Essie was with said, "You should really stop speaking to that girl. She acts like she doesn't like you." The others agreed. Essie thought to herself for a second but then she said, "I saved her life. Why wouldn't she like me?" After school, Essie and her friends met to walk to the bus stop. Essie spotted Jeanie and her friends and ran to catch up with her. The other girls watched as Essie got Jeanie's attention and said something. Jeanie looked annoyed, then yelled at Essie and stormed off with her friends in tow. Essie's friend met her halfway and asked what happened. "I don't know! That girl is mean. I was only trying to be friends with her." "Well, you might as well leave it alone, because she doesn't care about being friends with you." "I see that now," Essie said sadly.

A couple of days went by, and Essie stopped trying to talk to Jeanie.

She moved on, making it apparent that she was ignoring Jeanie and her friends. Essie and her friends had even come up with a name for Jeanie's group: the DPBs (Dirty Project B****s), because of where they came from and how they dressed. Jeanie and her friends lived in the same projects, dressed alike, and shared the same lingo. It wasn't just Jeanie and her friends that came from those projects; almost the entire school did since it was only ten minutes away from the projects.

One Saturday, Essie and her girls were hanging out at the back of the Barn. Since she was older, she was able to stay out later than usual. All her friends knew she liked to hang out there after-hours, but they weren't as bold as Essie and didn't try to sneak out.

They would pay some of the Barn patrons to get them cigarettes and drinks. They were all from the neighborhood, and they knew who they could ask—usually a guy named Larry who was the town handyman. Any time someone needed some work done on their house or car, they would get Larry to do it. Larry liked to drink and hang around the Barn. He was very talented, but he didn't understand the gift inside him. A product of his circumstances, he made a living by doing odd jobs for the town folks. Some would pay him cash, and some would buy him alcohol and cigarettes.

"There he is." One of Essie's friends pointed at Larry, who was on his way into the Barn. "Aye, Larry," they called. He smiled as he made his way over to Essie and the girls. "What's up, young ladies? How may I be of service to you today?" Larry said, making a gesture like he was tipping his hat. They began pooling their money. One of the girls in the group, Angel, never had money to buy anything but the group understood and didn't usually hold it against her. They would talk about her behind her back but always made sure to look out for her.

"Get me two medium cups of White Polk." "Get me one too, Larry!" "Me too!" They all chimed in, giving Larry the money for their drinks plus what he charged to purchase for them. "I want a cigarette too," said Angel. They all looked at her, thinking the same thing...if you want a cigarette buy one...but she never had any money. No one responded and she said, "So y'all ain't gon' buy me no cigarette?" as if they all owed her something. "I don't want no cigarette, so I ain't buying none," one of them said, while Essie and the other girl continued to ignore her. Larry smirked and walked off saying, "Beggars can't be choosers." Angel frowned but wasn't offended, because she didn't quite catch what he was saying.

A few minutes later, Larry came back with their drinks. He handed one to each of them but hesitated when Angel reached for hers. "Did you buy one of these, Li'l Sis?" She frowned again. Essie said, "Yeah. She bought one." Larry handed her a drink. "Where's the Kool-Aid, Angel?" Essie asked. Angel pulled a pack of grape Kool-Aid from her pocket, and they all poured some into their drink. They sipped, laughed, and hung out, enjoying each other's company.

Later that night, Essie was at home, pondering whether she should go back out. The house was always quiet now, as her older siblings were grown and doing their own thing. Sara had moved to another city in Louisiana when she ran off with one of the Montgomery boys last year, and no one had heard from her since she left. She had never really kept in touch with the family even when she was still living in the house.

Naomi got a full-ride scholarship to college and stayed at school for two years, then dropped out and moved back home. She was smart and resourceful, and her parents never worried about her even when she talked to them about dropping out of college. Naomi stayed in the house for a few months after she came home. She worked a good job, so she had enough money for her own place. She only lived a few blocks away from her family's home because she wanted to stay close. She had a small one-bedroom apartment that was on top of the local store.

Andon was still in the Navy. He had met a woman and was engaged to be married. He hadn't been home in a few years but planned to bring his fiancée home to meet his family soon. The baby boy was still at home. He was eleven years old now and in the sixth grade. Dad was home a lot now and spent a lot of time with him. Once, he took him to work with him and he came home talking about how he had played with his brother. Dad said one of his work buddies had his son at the Mill that day too, and the two played and called each other brothers.

Essie decided to go to the Barn. Her buzz from earlier had worn off, and she wanted another one. She didn't even bother going to her usual spot—she just hung out at the back of the Barn, waiting until she saw someone who could buy her a drink. After hanging around for about an hour and seeing no one she trusted, she went down to her spot. About fifteen minutes passed, and she heard someone say, "Hey, Essie." Essie turned around and to her surprise, it was Jeanie.

Essie glared at her and turned her attention back to the window. "I know I'm probably the last person you want to see right now but…" Essie cut her off and said, "You're right. Now move on!" Jeanie sat down on the top step. "That night we met, my mother got hurt." Essie sighed and rolled her eyes, ignoring Jeanie.

Jeanie continued; "She had been gone for like nine days. She leaves a lot and will be gone for months sometimes. But when she came back this time, she was hurt. Her face was bruised, and one of her eyes was closed and swollen. Her mouth was bleeding, and she had blood all over her clothes. She came into the house screaming and holding her stomach. It looked like blood was coming from her stomach. I tried to help her, but she kept calling Jennifer. I was going to go next door to call for help, but she told me to go get Jennifer. I didn't want to tell her Jenn was working here so I came to get her and ran into you. It's a secret that Jenn works here. If anyone knew then my mama would be in trouble. We alright at our house, you know. People wouldn't understand, but we be good. We don't need nobody coming from the outside, trying to control what we got going on." Essie was looking at Jeanie, confused. "What do you mean?" she asked. "I got six brothers and sisters. None of our daddies are around. My momma always be on some stuff. So, we gotta take care of ourselves. Jenn dropped out of school a while ago to take care of us…to make sure we can have some kind of normal. You know what I'm saying? So, when I saw you at school, I had to act like I didn't know you, because I would have to explain how we met." Essie realized what Jeanie was saying. "Oh! Okay, I get it now," she said. "So, Jenn is really like y'all's mama? Jeanie said, "Yep." "Ain't Jenn grown though?" "She is now; she only just made eighteen," Jeanie said. "But she has been taking care of us for at least three years now. My baby brother is three years old, and my mama ain't start messing up 'til after he was born. His dad got her hooked on drugs, and she ain't been right since. Jenn had to step up for us or all of us would have gone to an orphanage or something." Essie settled; like she got where Jeanie was coming from. Then she looked at Jeanie and asked; "What are you doing out here now?" Jeanie said, "I was hoping to find you so I could explain why I acted the way I did when I saw you at school." "Oh. Okay, that's cool." Essie seemed to loosen her stance. "You're cool, Jeanie. Thanks for that. Your sister knows you out here?" "Nope," Jeanie said. "Do you smoke?" She pulled a joint from her pocket. Essie looked content. Although she'd never smoked weed before, this was the start of Essie and Jeanie's life-long friendship.

Two years later...

Essie was graduating from high school, and she couldn't have been more excited. Although she had big plans, some things would end up taking longer than she anticipated. Essie and the entire class of Bremar High School 1962 lined up according to their last names to get ready to walk across the stage and accept their diplomas. Essie's family was sitting there excited and waiting to see her grace the stage. Naomi was there, the baby boy, Mama, and Andon Jr. and his fiancée, who was Korean. He thought it would be a good idea to bring her to the graduation so everyone could meet her. Essie's best friend, Jeanie, was also there; she was eight months pregnant and was more excited for Essie than Essie was for herself. Essie wasn't expecting her sister Sara to be there because no one even knew where she was or seemed to care. She did expect her dad to be there, but he wasn't.

CHAPTER
SIX

"YEAH, honey, my boss wants me to work on this special project next Friday between 10 am and 2 pm and then we plan to go out to eat and have a few drinks. Did you forget about my doctor's appointment that day? You know, I don't have nobody else to go with me." He looked devastated and so disappointed. She noticed it and began to cry because she knew how much of a burden she had become. "I'm so sorry, baby. I'm sorry. I ain't pick this, it picked me. You all I have." He was saddened by his wife's sadness but even more so by the diagnosis and how their whole life shifted in a matter of minutes. "Baby, no worries; I'll have to let them know I can't make it. He embraced his wife, and they cried together."

Later that evening, he looked out over the porch on the twelfth floor of the same housing projects where Jeanie and her family lived. They didn't stay in the same building; Jeanie's building was three buildings over which was about two blocks away, but he could see her building from his. He took a long sip of his beer and contemplated how he would tell Sarah that he would not be attending Essie's graduation. After a couple of beers, he finally got the courage to tell her. He grabbed his jacket off the kitchen chair, kissed his wife on the forehead, and said, "I'll be right back, Honey. Gotta grab something from the store."

He pulled up to the store and sat for a long time before he got out, then dialed the number on the payphone just outside of the store's main entrance.

Sarah was in the kitchen washing the dishes when the phone rang. "Hello?" "Hey, baby. What's going on?" Sarah smiled. "Hey, darling. How are you feeling?" "Well, I got some bad news. My boss's wife is sick with that cancer, you know." Sarah gasped. Andon Sr. continued the lie. "Yeah. He gon' be off for a few days, and he needs me to run the Mill, okay? I have to work the day of Baby Girl's graduation." "I don't understand," Sarah said. "Can't you get someone to cover for you just that one day? It's your daughter's graduation day! How can you even agree to this?" "Well, it does pay the bills, baby; and as much as I hate this, I got to." "This is BS, A.D., and you know it." Sarah never cussed unless she was really upset about something. "I guess you're expecting me to tell her." "Can you?" Sarah slammed the phone down.

Sarah wasn't buying his story. She knew about his secret family and thought that she had taken care of the issue…but what she had done made it much worse.

The Montgomery Plantation, seventy years ago…

Sarah had learned the secrets of voodoo long ago. They were only supposed to be used for the slave owners who'd treated them badly. When her grandmother taught it to her, she made her promise not to ever use it unless it was totally necessary; if she or her family were in danger or if it was the only solution. However, she had learned to use it to her advantage. Any time someone upset her, she would use it. Her enemies, including the Montgomerys, never knew why tragic things began to happen to their family. Isabelle Montgomery was the wife of John Montgomery Jr. who was the son of Father Montgomery, who was second heir to Father Montgomery. Mother Montgomery thought that their family had been cursed and thought all those things were isolated incidents. But Sarah's grandmother had taught her how to hurt people without laying a hand on them. She knew how to bring sickness and disease, harm, and danger. One time, Sarah put a hex on Isabelle Montgomery that turned all her hair gray, and then it fell out.

She started graying very slowly. She tried covering it up, but it began to turn fast; and one day, she awoke to a full head of gray hair.

Isabelle loved her hair. It was the perfect honey blond color and fell to her waist. Sarah wanted to hurt her…but she wanted her to suffer slowly. She put a spell on Isabelle because she had ordered her to the pig sty for three days. Everyone hated the pig sty because it was used to punish the slaves that misbehaved. Isabelle Montgomery had ordered Sarah there because she was jealous…she knew her husband wanted her. He was infatuated with her and sent for her often. He allowed Sarah special privileges and moved her entire family to one of the nicer houses on the property. The Montgomerys had a cluster of nicer cabins near the slave cabins. The Montgomerys would throw parties and hold secret meetings there, and they were often used for their trysts.

Some of the Montgomery men favored some of the slaves, both men and women. The night before Isabelle sent Sarah to the pig sty, she attempted to be intimate with her husband. No matter what she tried, he didn't seem to be interested, and she was hurt. She thought she was losing him, and the thought of her losing her husband to a slave made her ill. When her advances on her husband failed, she went into the bathroom and cried. Her husband heard her sobbing but didn't pay any attention to her. He got up from the bed, dressed, and left the house. When Isabelle heard the door slam, she got up and peeked out the window. Just as she thought, he was on his way to the cabin to be with Sarah. She was devastated and thought about killing her but knew she couldn't. She cried herself to sleep after trashing their bedroom in a bitter, jealous rage.

When Isabelle woke the next morning, she looked at how peacefully her husband was sleeping and at what a mess she had made in the bedroom. She dressed and went downstairs. She passed one of the maids and said, "Once Jonny awakens, go and clean up my bedroom," then went out to the cabin where Sarah and her family stayed. When she didn't see Sarah, she yelled, "Where is she?" Everyone looked nervous. "Who you looking for, ma'am?" one of the Lavenders asked.

She didn't even get the last word out before Isabelle spit in her face and kicked her in her stomach. "Don't play dumb with me. You know who I'm talking about." They all knew who she was talking about, but even though Isabelle was their owner, they wouldn't tell.

Sarah walked in the door, and Isabelle scowled at her and grabbed her by the hair. "You're coming with me." This made the rest of the family nervous, and the older ones began to cry. "Please, ma'am. Don't do this." Isabelle just looked at them in disgust. They thought she would kill Sarah, but their grandmother sat quietly and tried to calm everyone down. "She'll be back. Don't worry. She will be back." She began to rock back and forth and hummed a tune that brought peace to the atmosphere. Near the pig sty, Isabelle kicked and punched Sarah until she was tired, then made her strip naked and beat her. Sarah cried out, shaking from the pain that was being inflicted on her. She begged Isabelle, "Please, ma'am. Please stop." Sarah's face was bruised, and her nose and mouth were bleeding as Isabelle continued to brutalize her. Just when Sarah thought the beating was over, Isabelle got the bucket of water that was close by that was used to wash the pigs and the pig sty. She doused Sarah, drenching her naked bruised body. Then she got the whip that was used to punish the slaves who tried to escape or misbehaved.

It was long and much heavier than Isabelle anticipated, and she could barely lift it. She raised it once, but just before it landed on Sarah's back, she turned and grabbed Isabelle by the neck. With tears in her eyes and blood spewing from her face, she said, "I said stop! Please!" This shocked and terrified Isabelle. She dropped the whip and stared at Sarah, clutching her throat where she had grabbed her. She told Sarah, "This is your home from now on," and pointed to the door to the pig sty. "Don't come out of there until I say so." Sarah did as she was told.

Isabelle tried to catch her breath and slow her heartrate. She leaned on the side of the pig sty and took long deep breaths. John Jr. was leaving the house and noticed the slaves looking toward the pig sty, then saw his wife gripping the side of the building like she was having a heart attack. He asked one of the slaves what was going on and he answered,

"Mrs. Isabelle beat Sarah, but she couldn't whip her because Sarah choked her." He took delight in reporting the incident, because he knew what Sarah was to John Jr., and he was also proud that Sarah fought back. John Jr. was bothered, because he didn't want anything to happen to Sarah, but he couldn't show his emotions. Once he got to the buggy waiting to take him where he needed to go, he balled his fist in anger. "Where to, sir?" his driver asked.

Three days later, Isabelle's hair began to turn gray. She had her maid dye it back. She noticed huge chunks of graying hair every morning for two weeks straight. Every time she noticed it; she'd have the maid dye it again. Her maid warned her that dyeing her hair so often wasn't healthy, but Isabelle didn't care. She didn't want John Jr. to see her graying hair. Exactly one month later, Isabelle woke up screaming and woke her startled husband from his sleep. He looked up and saw that she was almost completely bald, except for patches of gray hair. She stayed locked in her room for a while, embarrassed at how she looked. She didn't have dinner with her family or interact with her children but stayed in her room with the curtains drawn and the lights off. She saw no one until Mother Montgomery forced her way in. She watched in shock as Isabelle took off her head scarf. Mother Montgomery left the room without saying anything. She returned with a card in her hand. "Get dressed, doll. We're going wig shopping."

Isabelle found a perfect match which brought a little of her confidence back, but she was still uneasy about not having any hair at all. She went to a doctor, hoping for a solution. She went back three times. The first two times, he sent her home, explaining that there wasn't anything he could do because he could not find a reason why her hair was falling out. The third time she went, she forced him to identify the problem. She would not leave his office without it. She was a Montgomery after all. She was part of a powerful family, and they got what they wanted when they wanted it. Because she was a Montgomery and they loved flaunting their power, she threatened the doctor telling him that she would make his life miserable if he didn't tell her what was wrong with her.

"You will diagnose me!" "Well, ma'am, you're healthy. I don't know what more you want," the doctor said. "You will diagnose me!" Isabelle yelled again. The doctor began to speak again, but she cut him off and repeated herself with tears in her eyes. Again, she said, "You will diagnose me!" This time Isabelle was weeping uncontrollably. Then it clicked, and the doctor then knew what he had to do.

Back at the Montgomery Plantation...

"The doctor said you have what?" Mother Montgomery asked with concern. "Oh Mother, it isn't contagious," said Isabelle, half smiling. "The doctor said I had a hair follicle infection. He gave me medicine to take there right in his office. He said that it wasn't available at the pharmacy because of its potency and my gosh, did it taste terrible. I had to brush my teeth repeatedly to get the awful taste out of my mouth," Isabelle said in a perfect southern accent. Mother Montgomery looked at her strangely, as though she didn't quite buy what her daughter-in-law was saying. Isabelle continued, "He said my condition should be improving soon." When her condition did not improve, the doctor lost his practice and was not able to practice medicine ever again in New Orleans.

Present day...

Sarah sat on her bed, fuming about A.D.'s decision not to attend Essie's graduation and feeling guilty. In some way, she felt responsible. She heard her grandmother say, "We are not supposed to use it to hurt our own people. You must remember that certain spells can curse you and those connected to you, so be careful." It was too late though. There was nothing she could do to reverse it. "What's done is done," she whispered to herself as she thought about how to deliver this news to Essie, but not before she went to her secret place; a hole in the bedroom floor that had been covered with a rug.

Sarah pulled the flooring back and grabbed a clay bowl that looked like incense had been burned in it. It had a large stick for crushing things. She got up and locked her bedroom door, pushing her dresser up to it in case someone tried to enter. She closed her curtains and lit three candles, then went to her drawer and pulled out some ladies' underwear. The underwear was old and torn in a few places. Sarah threw what was left of it into the bowl and set it on fire. She closed her eyes and started chanting. This went on for about a half an hour, until the underwear was burned to ash. When she opened her eyes, she looked tired and worn. She was sweating, and her nose was bleeding. This was what happened when she cursed someone. She left her room, took the bowl of ashes, and buried it in the backyard.

After the graduation ceremony, Essie met up with her family in the hallway of the school. Everyone was so happy for her, and they had brought balloons and gifts. As Essie hugged them, she noticed that her dad wasn't there. "Where is Daddy?" she asked. "He couldn't stay, baby. He had to go back to work, but he sent this for you." Sarah handed Essie a small gift box. It was a necklace with a heart-shaped pendant that read, "You will always be my baby girl." Essie was so pleased with the gift that she forgot how sad she was that he wasn't there.

The Lavender family went to lunch at a popular soul food joint. This place was a staple on the north side of New Orleans and was known for their tasty crawfish. They visited and laughed and enjoyed each other's company. Andon's fiancée got along well with the family. After dinner, they decided to go to the Barn to have drinks. Essie was now old enough to have a drink. The baby boy asked if he could go too, and they all chimed in, saying "No!" They dropped him off at home then headed to the Barn.

The family was enjoying themselves, dancing, drinking, and having a good time. Sarah sat at the bar, talking to the town folk, and Naomi was drunk by that time. Andon and his fiancée drank and chatted. Jeanie got Essie's attention, and they headed to the back of the Barn for a smoke break. While they were passing the joint back and forth, Essie saw Ray walk into the Barn. She looked as if she had seen a ghost. Jeanie asked her what was wrong. Following Essie's eyes, she noticed her looking at Ray and asked, "Who is that?" Essie ignored Jeanie and got up and followed Ray. Just as he began to walk toward Andon and his fiancée, Essie knocked over a chair in his path and he fell. Then she "accidentally" poured a pitcher of beer on him. Jeanie watched all of this. She was confused, but she started to laugh so hard that everyone else in the Barn began to laugh as well. Ray got up and looked at Essie, then ran out of the Barn, embarrassed. Andon just watched with a sigh of relief as he watched Ray leave. Everyone was ready to go home except for Naomi. Naomi wanted to stay and drink.

CHAPTER
SEVEN

A couple of days after Essie's graduation, Andon planned to go home for the weekend to spend time with his other family. He wanted to take them out to dinner and brought gifts for Sarah, the baby boy, and Essie. Charlotte, Andon's wife, had been diagnosed with cancer about nine months earlier. The cancer was very aggressive, and she would seem to be getting better and then get worse. She could barely do anything for herself, and her sister and her mother would come by to take care of her whenever Andon couldn't.

Charlotte and Andon Sr. met at the Mill where he worked. She was a bookkeeper and worked in the office. She would distribute the paychecks to the Mill employees every other Monday afternoon. She and Andon had gotten close over the years. They would talk about a lot of things. He thought that she was smart and beautiful, and he liked her point of view. He was attracted to her, but never really looked at her in a romantic way. Charlotte was very attracted to him and took it wrong when he befriended her. What was once an innocent friendship turned into a full-blown affair.

Charlotte knew Andon had a family, but she wanted to be married to him and have a family of her own. He tried to end the relationship many times, but Charlotte would not allow it. She didn't care that he had a family, and he made it clear to her that he would never leave them. She was jealous and manipulative and would get him drunk so that he couldn't drive home, just so he could stay with her all night. They spent a lot of time in hotels and had even slept together in his car. Charlotte would wait until the end of his shift to have her way with him because in her mind, she thought if she gave herself to him before he went home then he wouldn't have any energy left for Sarah.

When their relationship began, Charlotte still stayed at home with her parents and her older sister. She couldn't invite him to her house because their relationship was supposed to be a secret, but she told everyone who would listen that she was in a relationship with Andon Sr. Her family and friends were suspicious because no one had ever met him. Charlotte's mom and sister had an inside joke where they called Andon Sr. Charlotte's imaginary boyfriend. Whenever she talked about him, they would look at each other and laugh. Charlotte was head over heels in love with him; and after she lost her job at the Mill, she would show up after his shift. She would find any reason to pop up, bringing him dinner and buying him gifts just so she could see him. One evening, she showed up with a new camera. Before Andon Sr. knew what it was, she snapped a few pictures, even getting a picture with the two of them together. Now she had proof that her "boyfriend" really existed, and she couldn't wait to show off her pictures.

She knew he couldn't or wouldn't resist her advances, and she used that to her advantage. Andon Sr. was not in love with Charlotte. He loved what she could do to him; things that his beloved Sarah would not dare. Charlotte wore red lipstick and the same perfume whenever she and Andon Sr. were together. She'd intentionally kiss him in places where her lipstick would smudge. She would rub against him often so her scent would be on him. One night at the hotel, Charlotte tried to convince Andon Sr. to stay like she always did, however; he wasn't having it this time. He told her that he was worried that his wife suspected something because she'd started asking questions, and there was no way that he could stay the night this time. When he got up to go rinse off in the bathroom, Charlotte picked her panties up off the floor and put them in his work bag where he wouldn't notice them. She hoped that Sarah would find them and leave him, and she would finally have Andon Sr. to herself. Charlotte didn't know at the time that they had never married. Andon Sr. purposely left this little detail out of their conversations. But Charlotte got what she wanted, or so she thought. Sarah did find her panties, but she wasn't going to leave him. She had something else planned, not for Andon but for Charlotte...

"I got my own place now, Daddy," Charlotte said to Andon after popping up at the Mill after his shift one night. "Now you can come over to stay whenever you want." Andon said, "Oh yeah? That's good." "I got something for you," she said and handed him a small box with a string tied in a bow. He took the box and opened it. It was a key to her place. Andon asked, "What is this for?" She laughed like he was joking. "It's your key, silly. Your key to my house." "Where is it?" he asked. "It's in the Shallow Point Housing Projects. Let's go see it," she said. Andon was tired after a long shift, but he went anyway.

When they got there, he was intrigued by the atmosphere. He had heard about the projects but never thought he would visit. It was late but people were still out hanging, drinking, and smoking, and it looked as if everyone was having a good time. The music was blaring, and people were dancing and enjoying one another. He smiled at how everyone got along. It reminded him of his time in Haiti with his own family. They got to Charlotte's building and took the elevator to the 12th floor. Once off the elevator, they walked down a long porch where they could look out and see the city for miles. He loved the scenery and started thinking to himself that visiting from time to time wouldn't be so bad. Walking through Charlotte's apartment, he noticed how small it was. It was much smaller than the house he shared with Sarah and his children, but he liked it.

Andon pulled up to his parking spot in the back of the house. He'd gone shopping before coming home because of the guilt he felt for missing Essie's graduation, cheating, and not being there for his son, and he came bearing gifts. He used his key to get through the back door and was relieved when he saw the house was quiet. It was summer, and everyone was out enjoying the evening. He got to the room he shared with Sarah and found her napping peacefully. He thought to himself, "She's so beautiful." He continued to watch her and realized how much he missed her. How much he loved her. He thought about his dealings with Charlotte and just wanted to cry. He thought to himself, "What have I done? What am I going to do?" "Hey Dad!" he heard the baby boy yell as he rushed past the room. Sarah sat up with a look of disdain on her face. "What are you doing here?" she asked. "What you mean, baby? I live here!" "Oh, do you now? Stop running through here, boy! This ain't no barn!" Sarah yelled. Baby Boy ignored her and continued outside.

"Look what I bought you, baby…" The hopeful, enthusiastic look on his face changed to guilt and shame.

"You think you can waltz yourself in here with gifts and think everything is okay. Am I supposed to say nothing about you missing Essie's graduation? Am I supposed to say nothing about how I don't know if you live here or not? Should I continue to keep quiet about your mistress? It's clear to me that that's where you'd rather be." "That's not true. It ain't like that." As they argued back and forth, Essie and Jeanie came in and heard it all. They stood there stunned; Essie because she had just found out that her dad was cheating and missed her graduation because of it, and Jeanie because in all the years she had known Essie, she had never met her father, but now she realized that she had seen him in her neighborhood with Charlotte.

"I never meant to hurt you, baby. You know I love you and my family." Sarah was angry. "You don't love us, you love *her!*" she yelled. When he didn't deny his love for Charlotte, Sarah seethed with anger. She convinced herself that Andon was defending his mistress and began to sweat and speak in Haitian Creole. She knew that what she was about to say shouldn't be heard by anyone else, and as she continued to speak, Andon's eyes welled up, and the look of guilt and shame in his eyes became shock, anger, and disbelief. The tears began to run down his face as he whispered, "You did this to her?"

Essie and Jeanie stood there looking at them. Sarah, not realizing they weren't alone, said, "Did you think I would allow you to get away with that?" with a look no one had ever seen and a tone that no one had ever heard. "Did you?" she asked, like she was waiting for an answer. Then she laughed out loud, but her face told a different story. Andon put the rest of the gifts he had in his hand on the floor and walked out the back door past Essie and Jeanie as though they weren't there. Essie was staring at her mother in shock, not really grasping what had just happened. The look on her mother's face told her that something very horrible had just gone down right before her very eyes.

One month later...

"Where do you want this?" Essie asked Jeanie, holding a box filled with household products. "Well, it does say 'kitchen' right on the side of the box. You just graduated high school, right?" Jeanie said sarcastically. She and Essie laughed. "I didn't see it, preggo. You better be glad I care about my nephew, otherwise you'd be moving your own stuff. How did you end up with all this stuff anyway?" Essie asked as she set the box down in the kitchen. "I knew I'd be getting my own apartment soon. When you get pregnant, they give you your own apartment. Jenn had gone and applied for me when I was three months along. They said it could take up to six months, so she thought I would have it by the time I have the baby, and it all worked out. I have been saving up and buying stuff for the house. I didn't buy anything for the other room though." "That's so cool how Jenn always makes sure she looks out for y'all," Essie said. "Yep. I love her so much. I don't know what I would do without her." Jeanie replied. "But I didn't buy anything for the other room because I wanted to know if you would move in with me." Essie said, "That's nice of you Jean, but I'll have to pass."

Jeanie looked confused, because she thought that it would be perfect for them. Essie felt the opposite. Essie secretly loathed Jeanie's neigh-borhood, but she would never tell Jeanie that. "I don't want to leave my brother alone there, you know. Especially after finding that stuff out about my mom. I don't really trust her now, plus my job is closer to home. Thank you for thinking about me, but now ain't a good time." Essie saw the disappointment on Jeanie's face. "You know, I'll be here all the time. You might as well give me a key, because I'm always going to be here." she said. "Oh okay, I understand."

Jeanie went to her bedroom and came back with a joint. She took a puff and then passed it to Essie. "Boy, is my niece or nephew gon' be high as a giraffe when he gets here." They both laughed. "So, what's the deal with your mama and dad? Are they still fighting?" "My dad hasn't been back since that day, and we haven't heard from him in a while but that's normal. All my life he's been in and out of the house, working, supposedly. Both of them always said he was working; but after listening to them argue, I think he has another family. From the sound of it, my mother knew, and she finally did something." "She did something?" Jeanie asked, while blowing out smoke and trying to keep it in at the same time. "I used to hear rumors about my great-grandmother being a witch and putting spells on people, but I never really thought it was true." Jeanie was looking at Essie like she was crazy. "What do you mean? What kind of spells?" Essie shrugged. "I don't know. I used to hear folks around my house talk about voodoo and stuff, but I never really paid any attention to it. My great-grandmother Sarah started it all. She taught all her daughters, and it's been passed down. I remember when I was younger, I had a fight with one of my friends. She told me that her mother didn't want her to play with me because we were all witches. I never really understood that until now." "Do you know how?" "How what?" "You know, how to put spells on people," Jeanie said. "Girl, no!" "Shoot—you better learn. I can think of at least ten people for you" Jeanie said jokingly. They both laughed.

After having lunch and chopping down a few snacks, the girls finished unpacking. Essie decorated Jeanie's bathroom while Jeanie did the kitchen. Then they both unpacked Jeanie's bedroom and put together the bassinet that Jeanie had bought for the baby.

Essie got ready to leave. "Do you have to work tonight?" Jeanie asked. "Yes, I close with Mr. Melvin tonight and tomorrow, then I'm off for the next two days. I have my first math exam at school so I'm going to stay home and study and look out for my little brother." "Oh okay, I'll call you later. See you, Es."

CHAPTER
EIGHT

ESSIE was in her bedroom studying for her math test when her mother came in. "Hey, Baby Cakes," her mom said, hoping to make eye contact with her. "Hey," Essie said without looking up from her notebook. "Have you seen your brother?" Essie looked up. "No, actually I haven't. Is he out of school?" "Yes. He's been out for a few hours," Sarah said. "Did he have practice today?" Essie asked. "Oh. Yeah. Practice. What day is it?" "Monday," said Essie. By this time, she was looking at her mother like a crazy person. Essie thought to herself, "She knows darn well he's at practice." Her mother knew where her son was. She was just hoping for an exchange with Essie that made her feel like she still loved her, but she got nothing. Their relationship had changed since Essie witnessed the fight between her parents. Essie was disappointed in her dad, but she felt like it was all her mother's fault.

After Essie's shift later that evening...

Essie switched the sign to "Closed" as she securely pulled the front door tight, locking it from the inside. "Finally," she thought. Mr. Melvin was at the cash register, getting ready to count the inventory for the day. "How did we do today, Mr. Melvin?" Essie said. Mr. Melvin smiled and checked the receipt that he had just pulled with the numbers for the day. "We did pretty good, Baby Girl. Not bad at all."

Essie did what she usually did when she closed with Mr. Melvin; she prepared the store for the next day and headed out about an hour later. "Goodnight! I'm off tomorrow because I have to study for my math test, but I'll see you Tuesday." "Okay, Sweetheart. Be careful getting home." It was late but Essie never worried about working late. Her house was only a couple of blocks away, and she felt safe in her neighborhood. It was just before midnight, and she was almost at her street when she decided to stop at the Barn for a drink before going home.

The following day, Essie handed in her math exam to the professor, completely confident that she aced the test, and hopped on the bus to the other side of town where her little brother was playing varsity football. She got to the bleachers where she and her mom usually sat and saw her mom and Naomi sitting there. Essie was so happy to see her big sister. They embraced and cheered for their baby brother, who was the top scorer and led his team to victory. Throughout the game, Essie noticed her mother looking around with an uneasy look from time to time. She followed her eyes and noticed that she was watching a group of White boys. At one point, one of the boys looked over at Sarah with a smirk on his face, and he and Essie locked eyes. Sarah noticed it and then turned her head almost immediately. Essie kept staring at the young man until he finally turned his attention back to the game. She made a mental note of his face; there was something about it that made her feel like she needed to remember him.

After the game, Essie, Naomi, and their mother met her little brother on the field where the team was still celebrating. Everyone was crowded around him, cheering for him, and congratulating him on a good game. The three Lavender women just stood back and watched in awe, all of them overwhelmed with joy and being totally proud of him. Andontis ran over to them and said that he was going to hang out with his friends and that he would be home later. This made Sarah uneasy. "We're going to go to lunch to celebrate, Ma. I'll see you at home later." He kissed her on the cheek and hugged his sisters, then left with his friends, including the boy that Essie and her mom had been watching during the game.

He was much older than the other boys, but they seemed to know each other well. Essie's brother was the only Black boy in the group.

The Lavender women went to lunch and chatted about the latest things happening in their lives. Essie talked about being in college and how much she enjoyed learning about new and exciting things. She talked about Jeanie moving into her new apartment and the excitement they felt with the upcoming arrival of her baby. She told Naomi that she had gotten a promotion at work and was saving for her own place. Sarah looked surprised at first but quickly played it off saying, "That's great, Baby Cakes!" She felt so isolated by Essie. She never talked to her anymore or included her in any of her plans.

Naomi also talked about the good things happening in her life. She worked at an office as a secretary and accountant, and she practically ran the entire office. She was also a math tutor on the side. Naomi loved to teach but she was an African American, and that alone disqualified her from teaching. She had six children that she tutored for an hour each week. Her clients were wealthy White families, and she would travel to their homes for tutoring sessions. The word got out when Naomi helped a failing senior pass his classes and get into a prestigious college. The family was so impressed that they told all their friends about her and that was how she got started. Some of the families were horrible people who would treat Naomi badly, but they made sure she was paid because they knew she had what it took to help their kids pass. One family wouldn't allow Naomi to use their front door or their bathroom, but they paid her the most money. She figured it was a small price to pay.

Naomi also talked about the new man in her life. She said that they spent a lot of time together, and he was opening her mind to new and endless possibilities. She felt like they were totally in love and said that he was helping her find a house in a new neighborhood. "Oh. You're moving, baby?" Sarah asked. "Yes, soon enough Mama, but you will have a key and can visit whenever you want." "So, when can we meet him?" Essie asked. "Soon. Very soon," Naomi said.

After they were done eating and enjoying each other's company, Essie decided to go home with Naomi to stay the night. Naomi tried talking her out of it, but Essie was not accepting no for an answer. They made sure Sarah got home then headed to Naomi's apartment. It was a small, nice one bedroom. Her boyfriend apparently had nice taste, because she had expensive furniture, nice paintings, and other nice things.

"He got that for me," Naomi said to Essie while she was admiring a painting. "Wow! That's beautiful," said Essie. "Yes, he treats me really well. I love him so much." Throughout Essie's visit she had to hear about Naomi's new man. She grew tired of it but remained polite. She loved and missed her sister and was happy that she was finally happy. Later that evening as they were getting ready for bed, Naomi gave Essie a new pajama set to sleep in. Essie noticed that she had a lot of new things in her closet, coats, dresses, shoes, and other things. Naomi said that her boyfriend bought her all those nice things. "Every time he comes around, he has a gift for me," she gushed. The telephone rang and her eyes lit up. Essie saw this and ran to grab the phone. Naomi tried to stop her from answering but she was too quick.

"Hello, this is Essie…Hello? Hello? This is Naomi's phone. Can I help you?" "Oh hello. May I please speak to Naomi?" "You sure can," Essie said, giving the phone to Naomi. "Essie, can you excuse me for a second? Essie looked at her sister. "Go to the bedroom." Still confused, Essie stood there. "Go!" Naomi yelled. Essie did what she was told and went into the bedroom and closed the door, then opened it up just a crack so she could eavesdrop on Naomi's conversation. "Hello, Darling. How are you?" Naomi's voice trembled, then she went silent. She held the phone but didn't say anything else. "Okay, but when will I see…" Essie knew that he had hung up because Naomi couldn't finish her sentence.

After Naomi hung up the phone, she sobbed silently. Essie wanted to console her but closed the door and waited for Naomi to come to the bedroom to get her. The night was pleasant enough after that.

Naomi pretended that nothing was bothering her and talked about her boyfriend the entire night. She avoided any personal questions Essie asked, like where he stayed or what he did for a living. But when Essie asked if he was White, Naomi got quiet. "He's White?" Essie said. "Yes. He's White," Naomi answered. There was an awkward silence. "So, what did he say to you over the phone?" Essie asked. "Well, he was a little upset that I didn't tell him that you were coming over." "What? Nawni, why would you have to tell him when I come over? This is your house, right? Plus, I'm family. Why would he have a problem with that?" "No, it's not like that. He just wants all my time. He was mad because he couldn't come over to see me tonight." Naomi said with a fake snicker. Essie was not convinced at all and didn't mention that she saw Naomi cry after she finished talking to him.

Essie woke up to Naomi getting dressed for work. It was 6:30 am and she had to be at work at 9:00 am. "Hey Essie, breakfast is on the stove." "For real? You got up and cooked me breakfast? I could get used to this." Essie hopped out of bed and skipped to the kitchen. When Naomi said breakfast, Essie was expecting bacon, eggs, pancakes, and hash browns. What she got was one boiled egg, multigrain toast, and a slice of cantaloupe. "What's this?" Essie asked. Naomi, putting on makeup, stopped to see what Essie was talking about. "What's what?" "This," Essie said, staring at her breakfast like it was roadkill. Naomi laughed and said it was a perfectly balanced breakfast. "A perfectly balanced breakfast? I'll pass." Essie went back to Naomi's bedroom to lie down.

Naomi wondered why Essie wasn't getting dressed, so she asked her what she had planned for the day. She loved her sister, but she wanted her out. "Well, I kind of wanted to stick around here for a while. I don't have class today, but I have to be at work at 3:00 pm. Is it okay?" "No, it's not okay. Go home," Naomi imagined saying to Essie. "Sure, you can. Just be sure to lock the bottom lock when you leave."

Naomi left for work, and Essie went back to sleep. When she woke back up, it was 11:00 am. Essie went to the fridge to grab a bite to eat, and nothing looked appealing. She wondered what had happened to Naomi's tastebuds, because nothing in the fridge looked edible. She looked in the freezer and saw that Naomi had crawfish and decided to help herself. She made enough for Naomi too. She felt accomplished, like she had done a good deed. She put her sister's plate on the counter with a note that said, "Specially made for you," with a heart. Essie also helped herself to some of Naomi's clothing. She felt she would be doing her sister a favor by not taking any of her new items, so she grabbed a pair of Naomi's blue jeans and a very nice cashmere sweater that she put on over a T-shirt that she also took from Naomi's drawer. She couldn't fit into Naomi's shoes, but she did borrow a necklace. Essie wasn't into makeup, but she put on some of Naomi's lipstick and went to work. Before she left, she did a do over. She made sure she cleaned up after herself. She straightened up a bit, made up Naomi's bed, cleaned the kitchen, and left. She doubled back to make sure the bottom lock was on.

Essie had a great day at work. She got so many compliments about her clothes and a couple of their customers complimented the necklace she was wearing. One woman took a special interest in the necklace, indicating that it was a White woman's taste. Essie just shrugged it off. After her shift, she decided to go back to Naomi's house. Naomi was home, and she was cleaning. When she answered the door and saw that it was Essie, she was furious. First, she was annoyed because Essie was back at her house; but she was even more irritated that Essie had on all her clothes. "Essie, why do you have my clothes on?" Essie didn't catch on to how upset Naomi was at first and tried to butter her up by saying, "Because you're my big sister with style and class, and I want to be…" Before she could finish her sentence, Naomi pushed her away so hard that she almost fell to the floor. "These are my things, Essie! How dare you go in my stuff and just help yourself! I work hard to maintain my things! Don't ever just go into my stuff. EVER!"

"Okay, okay," Essie said. "I didn't think it was such a big deal. I'll get it cleaned and get it back to you." "No, you won't. Take it off." Essie hesitated because she wanted to go show off. "Now!" Naomi shouted. This hurt Essie's feelings. On the way to the bedroom, Naomi noticed she had on the necklace. That necklace was special to Naomi. She never wore it out. She only put in on when her man came to see her. He requested that she had it on only when he came. This sent Naomi into a rage. "Essie, if you don't take off my necklace, I will kill you!" Essie did as she was told. She was so hurt. She couldn't understand why Naomi was being so mean. She did consider that she just put on her clothes and her necklace without asking so she could not be totally upset with her because it was her fault. She just noticed a difference in Naomi. Everything about her sister was different—the way she talked and carried herself was different. Naomi was never a neat freak, but she cleaned and scrubbed like her house was dirty when it wasn't. She treated Essie like she was anything but her sister. Then Essie remembered the telephone call that Naomi had gotten the night before and thought that maybe this new Naomi was the product of having a new man who was White. As Essie left, she noticed the crawfish she had prepared for Naomi was in a bag in the garbage. On the walk home, Essie cried. At one point, she had to stop and take a breath because she couldn't control her tears. No one stopped to ask what was wrong or appeared to be concerned at all. Not that Essie cared. She hoped that folks would leave her be and not ask her anything. In this part of town, no one really knew Essie. It wasn't far from where she lived, but she knew no one and no one knew her. Naomi was the only person from this place she knew; and at this point, she wasn't even sure who Naomi was anymore.

Essie didn't want to talk to her mom about what had happened, so she took the bus to Jeanie's apartment. She had a key to Jeanie's house, so she let herself in. Jeanie's son was now eight months old. He was playing in his playpen, and Jeanie was sitting on the couch watching TV. Essie could smell that Jeanie had been smoking reefer. She smoked too but not as much as Jeanie. She desperately wanted to at that point, especially after what had just happened. Jeanie looked up smiling but then looked concerned because she could tell that Essie had been crying. "What's wrong, Essie?" she asked. Essie sat down next to her and took a deep breath; and before she got a word out, Jeanie handed her a joint and a lighter. "Here. It looks like you might need this." Essie told Jeanie what happened while they smoked.

Sarah was in her room, lying in her bed. She wasn't tired—she was just lying there. The house was so quiet she could have heard a pin drop. She was thinking about her life and how things were at the present time. All her kids were grown or growing up, and the father of her children didn't want anything to do with her. Essie loved and respected her, but she didn't engage much. Her youngest son, Andontis, was in and out of the house and never really spent any time with her. She felt alone and disregarded. She lay there, contemplating her actions and how she had caused some of this isolation. "I was wrong. I know it. I *am* wrong. I know it. 'This will have consequences if someone dies—keep this in mind.'" She heard the voice of her grandmother. Then she cried until she fell asleep.

"I can't believe Naomi would do that and then a White man at that? That is so foul," Jeanie said. "But then again, you know Naomi has always been a little bit dense." "Dense?" Essie looked at Jeanie like she had lost her mind. "I mean, come on, Es. To be honest, you are the only one in that family that seems to have any sense. The rest of them act like something is wrong with them. Even your ma…" Before she got that last part out, Essie stopped her, saying, "Watch it, Jeanie. That's still my family, and I won't allow you to continue to talk about them like that. No one's family is perfect, including yours. Jeanie then looked at Essie with a smirk, waved her off, and said, "Alright." Jeanie and Essie were good friends, but Essie noticed all the snide remarks she made, like what she just said about her family. Jeanie talked about how Essie dressed, how she talked, how she walked. She talked about where Essie worked, even though she didn't have a job herself. She received public assistance from the time she found out she was pregnant with the first baby, and that's basically all she had done. She hadn't completed high school either. She gave her first daughter to Jennifer so she could finish school but got pregnant again her senior year and dropped out. Essie tried encouraging Jeanie, but she was never interested in accomplishing anything. Essie even offered to help her get hired at the store where she worked and tried convincing Jeanie to get her GED, but Jeanie rejected it all, never giving a reasonable explanation. She would always have something negative to say, like she couldn't see herself "working in some raggedy run-down store" or a GED wasn't a "real diploma." She shot down every idea Essie had about improving herself. Essie had come to realize that even though they were friends, they were growing in different directions "Well, I'm going to go," Essie said. She picked up her things and left. She didn't say goodbye or even pick up Jeanie's son and hug him goodbye, which was something she had always done before leaving.

Three months later...

Naomi couldn't understand why she was so sick. She took good care or herself and made sure she stuck to a healthy diet. It had come upon her suddenly—she was fine at first but the next second, she was puking all over the place. Right before she had gotten sick, she was getting ready for a night with her man, cleaning her house excessively. She had the cleaning solution that her man had recommended—he told Naomi that it was the only thing he wanted to smell in her apartment. She used it in every room, but now it made her sick. She continued to use it even though she couldn't stand the smell of it anymore. Naomi continued to clean; and every time she got a whiff of that cleaning solution, she would vomit. Repeatedly, she used it because she knew she needed to have the house clean and smelling right. She could barely get done with one room before she was vomiting again. She only had a couple of hours before he got there, and she absolutely had to have her house cleaned. She grew weak; her head was pounding, and she couldn't shake the nausea. She went to her bedroom to lie down just for a second, thinking this would help her feel better. As soon as she lay down, she fell asleep and drifted into a dream about the first time he put his hands on her. When he got to her house, Naomi would take his coat and hat to her closet. This time, he did it himself. Naomi tried to save herself the embarrassment. "No, I got it," he told her, and as soon as he opened the closet door, everything that she had stuffed in it fell out. Naomi always wanted to impress him; but this time, she didn't have enough time to organize her closet. He looked at her, seething with anger, and motioned her to come closer. She did what he asked. She thought that he would hold and caress her and tell her that the mess was fine and that she didn't have to be embarrassed. Instead, he grabbed her by the back of her neck and forced her head down until her face was so close to the mess from the closet that she could kiss it. "What is this?" he asked. "What is it?" he yelled louder. Before Naomi could answer him, he grabbed her hair so firmly that she cried out. Fisting her hair, he grabbed her mouth, squeezing her jawline together with the other hand so tightly that her teeth cut through her cheeks and her mouth started to bleed. "I'm not accustomed to filth," he said. "Do you understand?" Naomi sobbed and shook her head up and down and far as she could because he still had her hair and cupped her mouth. He loosened his grip. "Good. Now clean it up." Naomi felt like she just had an encounter with the devil himself.

Naomi woke up. She hadn't slept very long. She looked for something to cover her nose so that she wouldn't continue to get sick while she cleaned. She was finally able to clean up her house and then she went to bathe. She cleaned herself in the same manner as she did her house. Profusely, excessively scrubbing every inch of herself. The bath soothed her nausea; but the minute she got out of the bathtub; she threw up again, more violently than before. She was so weak that she had to lay down because she felt as if she was about to faint. She knew she needed to clean the bathroom again. There was water all over the floor. The underwear that she'd worn that day was on the floor and she didn't bother flushing the toilet where she had vomited.

Naomi woke up on the bathroom floor. What she thought was a ten-minute nap was actually six hours. She panicked. She looked outside and it was pitch black—the middle of the night. The clock on her kitchen wall read 1:11 am. She looked around her house, confused.

She was then reminded of why she had fallen asleep and ran to her bathroom and was greeted by the vomit that she left in the toilet. Her instincts made her turn her head, and she vomited in the bathroom sink. Her apartment wasn't that big, but she searched around frantically like she lost something. She wondered whether he had come…if he did, he would have seen the mess she left. "If he did, then why didn't he wake me up?" she thought. Clearly, he would have been upset. Then she felt a slight sense of relief, thinking about what might have happened if he had come and seen the mess she made. But what if he came, saw the mess, saw her sleeping, and left? This sent Naomi into a crying fit…and then she threw up again.

It had been three weeks since Naomi had heard from him. They usually saw each other at least twice a week. If it happened three times, Naomi considered herself lucky. Naomi hadn't seen or heard from him, and she didn't know what to make of it. She had no way of contacting him. She wouldn't dare go to his work or show up to his house… that would be a death wish. Two more weeks passed, and Naomi was stressed and overwhelmed with crazy emotions. One second, she would imagine them together: happily married with children in a nice big house with a white picket fence. The next, she was crying uncontrollably, wondering what was happening in her life.

"Congratulations, Ms. Lavender, you're (the doctor paused and looked over Naomi's chart) seven weeks pregnant." Naomi sat there, processing what she'd just heard him say. The doctor stared at her wondering if she had heard him. Before he repeated himself, Naomi said, "I heard you," and put her hand up. Then she asked, "Are you sure?" "Yes. With the symptoms you've reported and your last period, that puts you at exactly seven weeks. You will be two months in six days. Shall we begin prenatal care?"

The following week...

"That's wonderful darling," Sarah said after hearing the news. "I hope it's a girl." "It really doesn't matter to me," Naomi said, "as long as the baby is healthy." Sarah was so excited to be a grandmother. She hoped and prayed for a girl, literally. *Dear Lord, I come to you in your son Jesus' Name. Lord, you know what we need before we even ask. I am asking you to go before us, before Naomi and the father of the child, clearing the way and settling the score. You are God Almighty, and you can do anything but fail. You fight on our behalf, and you make us victorious. We need you God...we need you....*

NINE

ESSIE was startled out of her sleep, as her mother sat at the edge of her bed. "I'm sorry, Essie. I didn't mean to scare you. It's just that I've been trying to catch you. You're so busy these days that I barely get the chance to see you." "What is it, Ma?" Essie said. "Well, I know you and your sister aren't really seeing eye to eye, but I have some good news. She's pregnant!" "Who's pregnant?" Essie asked. "Naomi! Naomi's pregnant. She's two months along." Before Essie could say anything else, her mother embraced her, hugging her tightly. She was very excited to be a grandmother. Essie asked, "Is she pregnant by that guy she was dating a few months ago?" "I didn't ask. Why?" Essie pulled her covers up and laid back down and her mom left the room. It had been a while since she and Essie had a conversation or embraced each other. Even though it was more of her doing, she felt accomplished and happy that she got a chance to talk to and hug her baby girl. Meanwhile, Essie lay in bed, wide awake and worried about her big sister.

Another month had gone by since Naomi last saw her man. She was getting used to being pregnant. In fact, she enjoyed it and couldn't wait to be a mom. She had gotten past the horrible morning sickness, and her life was going well. Naomi couldn't get used to him not being involved in what could be an amazing experience for both of them. "Surely, he would be happy that I am pregnant," she thought. Even with all the wonderful things happening in Naomi's life, it didn't stop her from feeling hurt, isolated, and rejected; not able to talk to him and tell him she was pregnant. She was hopeful though. She still prepared for him to come over. Every week, she went through her routine, hoping and praying that he would show up. He never did.

Naomi was five months along, and there was still no word from him. Sitting at her mom's kitchen table while Sarah prepared her something to eat, she said to herself, "Is he dead?" Her mother heard her but pretended that she didn't. "Do you think he's dead?" Sarah turned to face her. "Who is dead?"

Naomi told her mother everything about the relationship. Essie came in while they were talking. She grabbed a chair and sat next to Naomi, holding her hand and rubbing her back. She saw that Naomi was troubled. They had been cordial, at least, but their relationship hadn't been the same since they had that big fight. Sarah was furious but also afraid for her daughter after hearing what Naomi suffered through. She was afraid because she had a feeling that the child's father was a powerful White man or the son of a powerful White man. She knew that Naomi would be in danger if that were the case. Naomi never mentioned whether he was, and Essie never told her but listening to Naomi talk about him and their relationship, it just made sense.

"Naomi, why don't you come home for a while? You could stay in my room if you don't want to go back in the room with Essie." "No, Ma. I'm going home. Don't worry—I'll be fine. You know once you get used to having your own space, you appreciate it more and prefer to sleep in your own bed rather than anywhere else." Naomi chuckled to herself while Sarah and Essie looked at her, then at each other while she went to the restroom for the fifth time in an hour. The real reason Naomi didn't want to stay was she didn't want to miss him just in case he decided to come by.

The day of Essie and Naomi's fight...

"Hey, you!" Naomi's neighbor called out to Essie while she was leaving her house. Essie wasn't in the mood for small talk. She was fuming after the argument she had just had with her sister. Essie looked at the lady who was older, much older. She had a full head of gray hair pulled back in a bun and she wore glasses. Essie pointed at herself, and the lady shook her head yes, motioning her to come closer. She got close enough for the lady to whisper, "He beats her, you know." "What?" Essie said. Then the lady put her finger over her own lips, telling Essie not to say anything and went back to her apartment. Essie stood there not knowing what she should do. Watching her sister come from the bathroom, she had almost cried. She couldn't understand how anyone could mistreat Naomi. She was beautiful, smart, and independent. She was so nice to everyone and had never had any enemies. How could he treat her this way? Essie wanted to tell their mother what Naomi's neighbor told her that day, but she decided against it. She did offer to go home with Naomi. Naomi declined.

After Naomi got home, she soaked in the bathtub and thought about him. She thought about them being together; herself, him, and their baby. She thought about him arriving home after work. She imagined having his dinner warm and ready for him when he got in the door. She pictured him removing his hat and coat and placing his keys on the countertop. She imagined him greeting her with a kiss and playing with their baby. She imagined them eating together, laughing, and talking. These thoughts made Naomi forget reality for all but a minute. She got out of the tub, sobbing loudly. All she could think about was being rejected, isolated, and alone. Then she had a flashback to the first time she felt pain like this. May 15th...

"Did you enjoy yourself tonight, Naomi?" James asked after he pulled over on a dark road. They had just enjoyed dinner and a movie. Naomi was completely smitten. After all, James could have any woman he wanted but he chose her. She felt a sense of pride in knowing that. After pulling over, he turned the radio station to set the mood. He pulled out a flask and took a swig, then offered it to Naomi. She declined at first; but with a little persuasion, she decided to go ahead and enjoy herself. A song was playing, and James sang along. She blushed as he rocked his head back and forth, snapping his fingers, glancing at her. She loved every minute of it. All the attention he gave her was something she'd always wanted. Then he moved closer and started to kiss her. Naomi had never been kissed before, so she was a little nervous. He whispered softly in her ear and told her to relax. He then started to pull her dress up and fondle her. She was very uncomfortable, but she did not stop him. He began to aggressively rub her while kissing on her neck. Naomi still didn't stop him. She thought maybe this is how things are supposed to go. She tried to pretend she knew what to do. But James already knew she was inexperienced which is the reason he chose her. He then let her seat back. This scared her because it happened abruptly. Before she knew it, he was on top of her. At this point Naomi felt smothered so she lightly pushed his chest as a gesture for him to move off her. He didn't. In fact, it excited him even more. He ripped her stockings and forced himself on her. "Turn around" he told her, and she did. Naomi didn't yell out although she wanted to. It all happened so fast but felt like it lasted forever. When James was done violating her, he continued to kiss and caress her. He asked her if she liked it. Naomi couldn't speak. She was in pain. She was embarrassed. She was afraid, but she never yelled, didn't fight, she never told anyone. James never said a thing to Naomi after this. He acted as if he didn't know her at all. This hurt Naomi the most. Not that he raped her, but the rejection she felt was much worse than that.

She cried herself to sleep.

Naomi got up the next morning determined to no longer be a victim. She had wasted enough time feeling sorry for herself. She was going to be a mother soon, and she had to stand up for herself. She decided to go find him and tell him about their baby and that they were going to be a family whether he liked it or not. She didn't understand where this courage came from—she felt fearless and unapologetic suddenly, and she liked it.

Naomi got dressed. She was even bold enough to wear some of the jewelry he had bought her. She knew exactly where he worked so she headed that way. When she got there, her courage was gone. She walked past his company at least six times before she walked in. The receptionist looked at her strangely because she was an African American woman, and they didn't work with many of them. "Hello. Are you lost?" "No," Naomi said. "May I speak with John?" John? "Does John have a last name?" the receptionist asked. Naomi froze, realizing that he had never told her his last name. "Ma'am?" the receptionist asked again because Naomi seemed to have blacked out. Naomi stuttered and said, "I don't have his last name, but he is a manager at this company." The receptionist looked at her and said, "I'm sorry, ma'am, but we have many men working here, and if you don't know his last name maybe you're at the wrong place." "No," Naomi said, "This is the right place. He works here. I met him here before, and I know he works here." Her eyes welled up with tears. The receptionist asked if she could get her some water. She then noticed that Naomi was expecting. She motioned her to a chair and said, "Please have a seat. I'll get you some water and then we will try and find this John, okay?" Naomi nodded. While she was sitting there, she watched as people came and went. All of them stared at her in disgust wondering who she was and why she was there. One of the men who looked like he was someone important asked her who was she and why was she there. Before she could answer, the receptionist came back with her water and told him that she was taking care of her.

The receptionist sat down next to Naomi and said, "I checked, and we have no one here named John." Naomi seemed to shrink and said, "Maybe I am mistaken." As she stood up to leave, she heard a familiar voice that stopped her in her tracks. "Good afternoon, Paula," he said to the receptionist. "Please send this priority to Dr. Charleston." Naomi turned and froze. She was happy to see him, but she was also afraid of what would happen. He turned to leave and saw Naomi. He did a double take and then brushed past her. She knew he was upset; but she was there, and she was determined to accomplish what she had set out to do. She walked toward him, and he stopped, fuming. The receptionist watched them warily. Naomi said, "Hi, John. We need to talk." He said, "I'm sorry, ma'am. Do I know you?" Naomi walked closer to him with tears in her eyes. "John? What do you mean? It's me, Naomi!" As she came closer, he moved further away. "You are mistaken, Miss. I am not the man you think you know," he said. Paula, the receptionist, got up and started guiding Naomi toward the exit.

Naomi felt defeated for a moment, then pushed Paula so hard that she almost fell. "Get out of my way. Oh, you don't know me, John? This is your baby I'm carrying. This is *our* baby. How can you not know me when I am carrying your child? Doesn't it seem strange? Doesn't it?" She looked around as if she were seeking validation from the people in the waiting room. Everyone stared at her. Most of them began to whisper, "Who is this nigger? She's crazy." "You're a liar and a cheat," Naomi yelled. "You know me, John." As the receptionist regained her composure, John said, "Get her out of here." Paula went to take Naomi's arm, and she looked at her and said, "Do. Not. Touch. Me." Paula stopped, and John said, "Call security. This lady is crazy. Then the man who had asked Naomi who she was earlier came out of his office and yelled, "Get this nigger out of here now!" The police arrived and dragged Naomi out, kicking and screaming. Once the office was quiet again, Paula said, "Are you okay, Sebastian?" He said that he was and told her to cancel his appointments for the day—he was going home.

Naomi sat in a cell for about four hours before they allowed her a phone call. She was uncomfortable, hungry, and nauseated, but no one seemed to care. She asked them several times if she could get something to eat because she was pregnant, but no one paid any attention. When she finally got her phone call, she called her mother's home, hoping she or Essie would be there to answer, but the phone rang and rang. Naomi tried to hang up and call back, but the officer stopped her and took her back to her cell. "When can I eat, sir? Will I get another phone call?" He pushed her back into the cell and locked it without answering her.

The following morning, Naomi was awakened by the sound of the cell door opening. She jumped up, feeling worse than she had the day before. It had been almost twenty-four hours since she had eaten. Her head was pounding, and her entire body ached. The security officer handed her a sandwich and a cup of water. Naomi knew she needed to eat for the baby, but it didn't stay down long, and she vomited it back up. She yelled for the guard, and when he got to the cell, he was angry that she had gotten sick. He yelled, "Hey, Meredith. Where's the mop? The pregnant nigger in cell seven just vomited all over the place." Another officer came to the cell with a roll of toilet paper and some cleaning solution. He grinned and said, "Meri is at lunch. She's going to clean up this mess on her own." They both laughed, and the guard handed Naomi the tissue and cleaning solution. Naomi asked, "What am I going to do with this?" "Clean up that mess!" the officer yelled. "You won't get your phone call until it's spotless."

CHAPTER
TEN

SARAH rushed into the house and went straight to the bathroom. Essie was at the kitchen table studying, and Andontis was in his parents' room talking on the telephone. He had a new girlfriend that he couldn't get enough of. Every chance he got he spent with her either in person or on the phone. "Whew! Oh, my goodness. I almost didn't make it," she said, walking to the kitchen sink to wash her hands.

"Hey, Essie, how was your day?" "It was good. The bus passed me by, so I had to walk home from Halston Street." "Really? It must have been a White bus driver. Is your brother here?" Essie nodded toward her bedroom. "Have you heard from Naomi?" Essie asked. Sarah said that she hadn't, and Essie said, "I was worried about her, so I stopped by her house and didn't get an answer. Her neighbor said that she hasn't been home in over a week. She also said she had seen a couple of strange guys hanging around their building like they were waiting for someone."

"This is not like Naomi," Sarah said, and she went into her bedroom. "Give me the phone, boy." He looked irritated. "I'm using it." Sarah snatched the phone out of his hand and hung up without saying a word. Then she dialed Naomi's number. She tried five times and didn't get an answer. "This worries me, Essie, especially after all that's happened." Now Essie was worried. "What should we do? Should we call the police?" "I don't think that will work. Let's go see if she is in the hospital. Maybe she has gone into labor early or something."

It had been three weeks since they last heard from Naomi, and Essie and Sarah were frightened. Sarah even called their dad to let him know. She was distraught because she didn't know whether her daughter was dead or alive.

Sarah debated with herself. She had vowed never to do it again, but she told herself she had to for this last time. She went to her backyard where she had buried her secret, then came back into the house and went to her bedroom, pushing her dresser drawer against the door so no one could interrupt. Essie walked in from class. She heard her mother in her room wailing and smelled something burning. She moved close to the door and leaned in to try to make sense out of what Sarah was saying. After a few minutes, the speaking slowed, and Essie heard Sarah push the dresser back. When she opened the door, she looked different. Her face was flushed, her eyes were red, and she had a little speck of blood seeping from her nose. Essie frowned and was about to ask what was wrong, but Sarah said, "She's in jail." "What? Who's in jail?" "Naomi. We need to go get her." Essie asked how she knew, but Sarah didn't answer.

After sitting in the waiting room for what seemed like forever, Naomi was released. Sarah jumped up to greet this frail frame with a baby bump. Naomi looked sick. She had lost weight, but her baby bump was much bigger than the last time they had seen her. Essie wanted to cry. She had never seen her sister look so lost, disappointed, and broken.

They got home and Naomi barely spoke. She didn't want to eat. She didn't want to talk. She just cried. She was thankful to be out of jail, but she was saddened by what had brought her to this point. Sarah drew her a bath, and Essie made them something to eat. Sarah went into their room, the room that Naomi used to share with Essie. "I'm running bath water for you, Dear." Naomi nodded. Sarah sat down and put her arms around her, and Naomi cried like a baby.

Two days had passed since Naomi was released from jail. She got up that morning and made herself some breakfast. After she had eaten, she decided to go home. Essie was at school, her mom was at work, and her brother was at practice. Naomi had begun to get her strength back, so she wanted to go to her home. At first, she felt like she couldn't, because Sebastian was all over her home. She knew it was over and that her house would be a constant reminder of him, so she had stayed away, but today she was ready.

She planned to clean and get rid of any evidence of him. She was hurt but she also felt a sense of relief; a release of all the hurt and pain that had surrounded their relationship and of the fear and condemnation that she had felt, knowing that he truly never loved her. Now she felt she could focus on herself and her baby. She rubbed her belly for the first time in a long time and vowed to love her baby unconditionally. She realized that it was best that her baby would never know its father, and she was glad that she didn't have to expose the baby to him.

Naomi was in her apartment, cleaning away any evidence of Sebastian. She was able to use the cleaning products that had made her sick. She had music playing and she felt peace all around her. She heard a knock on her door which startled her and then she remembered that she no longer needed to be afraid in her own home. It was her neighbor. She brought Naomi all the mail that was delivered while she was gone. Naomi had never really talked to her, but she smiled and said hello, then thanked her for bringing the mail. There was an awkward silence as they stood there staring at one another.

"Um, would you like to come in? I'm just cleaning up my place and getting used to being here again." "No thanks, honey. I'm on my way out. I heard your music and thought that you must be home and wanted to give you your mail." Naomi thanked her and before she closed the door, her neighbor embraced her. Naomi was taken back by it. Her neighbor said, "I'm so happy that you're alright. I was so worried about you." Naomi was going to try to pull away but instead she allowed it. She felt comforted as they embraced each other. Then the neighbor whispered, "You have more people that will love you and your baby than don't. Always remember that." "Yes, ma'am," Naomi said.

Naomi closed the door and started going through her mail. There were a bunch of bills and disconnection notices. There was a letter from one of her tutoring families, asking her to come back and offering her more money. She got a notice from her job indicating if she wasn't back by a certain time that she would be terminated. Naomi picked up her phone to call her job and the parents of the child she tutored, but it was disconnected. She planned to go talk to her boss and the students' parents, in the hope of keeping her jobs. She also had notices from her doctor. She had missed some important appointments, so she also planned to get to the doctor to check on the baby. Then she realized that she was tired and decided to take a nap.

Essie had just gotten home from work. She was exhausted. Sarah was in the kitchen preparing dinner, and her brother was in their mother's bedroom on the phone. Essie went straight to her bedroom to lie down. She fell asleep almost immediately. In her dream, she saw Naomi running through a field filled with beautiful flowers. It was a beautiful summer day. The sun was shining, and children were playing on a playground close by. Naomi noticed Essie and began to run towards her. Suddenly, clouds covered the sky and it started to get dark. The children on the playground froze and looked up at the sky. It began to pour down rain. It started to storm. Now thundering and lightning, the sky grew darker and darker. Essie turned her attention back to Naomi who was sinking into the mud. She looked afraid and cried out to Essie for help. Essie started running towards Naomi, but she couldn't run fast enough because she was also sinking. "Essie, Essie. Help me please!" Naomi cried, but Essie couldn't get to her. She looked over at the children on the playground who were holding hands in fear of the storm. Essie finally made it to the place where Naomi was, but she wasn't there. It was a huge muddy puddle. Essie began to dig through the mud in an attempt to save her sister. As she was digging, she looked at her hands and the mud turned into blood. Essie cried, "NAOMI!" Then she woke up.

Essie was troubled by her dream. She went into the bathroom to wash her face, then went to the kitchen where her brother was eating dinner. "Where's Ma?" He didn't answer but continued devouring his meal like it was his last. Essie went into her mother's room where she was sitting on her bed. "Hey, Ma. Have you talked to Naomi.?" "No, I haven't. I tried calling her earlier and her phone is off. What's wrong?" "Nothing," Essie said, then headed back to her bedroom.

When Essie got up the next day, she planned to go to Naomi's after work. After she closed the store, she headed to Naomi's home. Her neighbor was in the window as Essie walked up. She knocked but didn't get an answer. Remembering her dream, Essie became worried and started calling out Naomi's name in a panic. The neighbor opened her door and said, "She's in there. She's probably just sle-…" before she got the word out, Naomi opened the door, looking disheveled. "Essie, why are you beating on my door like that?" Essie was relieved to see her. "I'm sorry. I didn't know if you were here." Naomi appeared annoyed because she had woken her up. Essie noticed that Naomi had rearranged her apartment. She also noticed all the mail sitting on the table, disconnection notices and letters from her doctor. "Is everything okay?" she asked. "Yes," Naomi said. "I might have lost my job, but I'll be having the baby soon anyway." "Do you need money? I have some saved, and I got paid today. I can help out with some of your bills." You would do that for me, Essie? Thank you. I just need to pay the phone bill and buy groceries." Essie opened her bag and gave Naomi all the cash she had in her wallet. "I can give you more if you need it." "No, Essie. This is more than enough. Thank you so much, Sister. Do you want to go with me to the grocery store?" Essie nodded, and Naomi said she would be right back as she went to get dressed.

They returned to Naomi's and started putting away the groceries. "I wonder how Sara is doing. It's a shame we haven't seen or heard from her in so long," Essie said. "She made it very clear that she wanted nothing to do with us, so what can we do?" Naomi said. "Yeah, you're right. I just think that if she had given this place a chance, we all could have been so close. I miss her sometimes—I just hope she is okay." Naomi and Essie prepared dinner together, ate, and just enjoyed being together and appreciating their restored relationship. They talked about baby names and about going shopping after Naomi's doctor's appointment in a couple days. Essie planned to take the day off so she could go with her.

"Everything looks fine, Ms. Lavender. You're approximately thirty-one weeks, so you should be delivering a healthy baby in about two months or so. I need you to be sure to take your prenatal vitamins. You have lost a bit of weight, and your iron is rather low. Taking them will ensure that you and your baby will be healthy." "I'll be taking them every day. Should I eat first?" The doctor said to take the vitamins with breakfast and to drink orange juice to help with the taste. He told her to schedule another appointment with the receptionist for two weeks from now.

Essie was waiting for Naomi in the waiting area and watched as she walked to the front desk. She noticed how different she was walking; she looked unsteady, like she would tip over. Essie laughed to herself. Naomi scheduled her appointment, and they left the clinic.

"Are you hungry?" Essie asked Naomi. "Of course. I'm always hungry." They both laughed. The doctor's office was just a block over from Sebastian's office. Naomi knew a restaurant that was just across the street. She thought about avoiding it, but they had the best pancakes she had ever tasted. Sebastian would always bring her food from there, and it was where they met. As they headed to the restaurant, Essie noticed a shift in Naomi's energy. "You okay?" she asked. "I'm fine. This is where I met the baby's father," Naomi said. "He works right over there." Naomi pointed to the building across the street. "We don't have to eat here. We could go somewhere else if you want." "No, I'm fine. It just reminded me of him. I wouldn't miss this meal for the world."

They spent about two hours there and when they finished, Essie went to the register to pay. While Naomi was gathering her things, Sebastian walked in. She froze. He didn't see her at first. He stood behind Essie while she paid. He stared at Essie for a long time because she looked like Naomi and for a second, he thought it was her. His eyes followed Essie, and that's when he noticed Naomi standing there with her back turned. His entire face turned red as a fire hydrant. He ordered his meal to go then sat by the register and waited for his order.

Naomi tried to avoid making eye contact. Essie continued to talk, but Naomi couldn't hear anything she was saying. He stared at Naomi angrily, and she looked at him for a moment before turning her head. They left the restaurant and headed toward the bus stop. Naomi was sweating profusely; her heart was racing, and she couldn't catch her breath. "I think I'm going to be sick." Essie knew something was wrong; but before she could say anything, Naomi threw up. While she was bending over, she took off her sweater because she was so hot. Naomi grew weak and couldn't stand, and Essie helped her to the ground. "I can't breathe," Naomi said, panting. "Oh my God. What's wrong? Do you need some water?" "I don't know. I'm scared. I don't know what's wrong with me." Essie ran back to the restaurant. "Call the ambulance. My sister is sick, and she's pregnant." Sebastian was still waiting for his order. The lady at the cash register called an ambulance, and Essie went back out to Naomi. She sat there holding her in her arms and wiping the sweat off her forehead. Sebastian left the restaurant. He saw Naomi in distress but kept walking like he didn't know her; like she wasn't carrying his child.

"Ms. Lavender, I said two weeks not two hours," Naomi's doctor said jokingly. "I think you had a panic attack. Did something happen after you left?" Naomi knew exactly what happened. "No. We went out to eat, and I got sick shortly afterward." "It could have been something you ate, but it looks more like panic to me. Your heart rate increased, you were sweating, and you were short of breath. Those symptoms are not an indication of food poisoning. Are you sure nothing happened when you left here?" Naomi insisted that nothing had happened, and the doctor said that he was going to admit her for twenty-four hours so that she could be monitored. Naomi tried to tell him that it was not necessary, but he insisted.

Once she was settled, they allowed Essie in to see her. She embraced her and said, "I'm so glad you're okay. What did they say?" "They want to monitor me to make sure the baby is okay." "You said that was a good restaurant," Essie said. "It wasn't the food. I saw Sebastian. He was in the restaurant, standing behind you when you paid for our food." "Really?" Essie asked, shocked. "Yes. He was there, and I got so scared because the last time I saw him, he treated me like a stranger. I ignored him so I wouldn't feel like that again, but my emotions got the best of me, and I couldn't breathe." "Wow, Naomi. I wish I had noticed. Why didn't you say anything?" "I couldn't say anything." "Well, I'm just glad you're okay. Do you want me to stay?" No, you don't have to. Just go let Mama know where I am so she won't worry."

On the way home, Essie thought again about the dream she had and wondered if it was a sign of what had just happened.

CHAPTER
ELEVEN

ESSIE and Sarah were sitting at the kitchen table. Essie had just told her about the dream she had. "It was probably a message from our ancestors. We have people from our past that are watching over us." Essie was confused. "Don't worry," her mother said. "This is good for us." "Do you talk to them?" Essie asked. "Yes, I do, but only when I really need to." "Has there ever been a time that you really needed to?" Essie said. Sarah said yes that there had been times where she had to call on them. Essie asked if she could talk to them, and Sarah looked shocked. She said that she could, but not now.

The next day, Essie went to Naomi's house to pick up some clothes for her because she had vomited on the ones she was wearing. When Essie walked in, she felt like something wasn't right—like someone was watching her. Then she remembered the conversation she had with Sarah the day before and thought to herself, "Maybe it's my ancestors," She laughed out loud at that thought. Once Essie got Naomi's clothes and some snacks, she left and locked the door. On her way out, Naomi's neighbor looked out her door. "Hey there, young lady." "Hey," Essie said, but kept walking. "How is everything?" the neighbor asked. "Everything is okay. Thanks for asking." Essie didn't tell her that Naomi was in the hospital. After Essie had gone, the neighbor heard something in Naomi's apartment, but she knew no one was there. As she closed her door, she heard Naomi's door open. She peeked out, and saw two young

White men leaving Naomi's apartment. They both looked strange. She thought that they had been there with Essie. "Boy. The love for White men must run in their family," she said to herself as she closed the door.

As Essie, Sarah, and Naomi were leaving the hospital, they talked about what they wanted to eat. Sarah convinced Naomi to come to the house and let her cook for them so that they could eat together. Sarah always wanted her kids together, and this was the perfect opportunity. When they arrived at the house, Andontis was on his way out. He greeted them and rubbed Naomi's belly. "Where are you going?" Sarah asked. "I'm going to see my girlfriend." Sarah rolled her eyes and said, "He acts like he can't live without her. If he isn't on the phone with her, he is spending all of his time with her." Naomi said, "Well, Ma, you know how it is when you first start seeing someone…they are all you think about." Essie nodded. "When you find that person, they are the only one in the world you want to be with." "Yes, I know," Sarah said.

While Sarah was preparing dinner, her phone rang. She asked Essie to answer it. Naomi was in Essie's bedroom lying down, and Essie was working on homework. When she answered, she was pleasantly surprised by who was on the line.

"Hey, Andon!" she said excitedly. Andon talked to everyone in the house, even Naomi. He was doing well. He was still in the Navy, and he and his wife were expecting their second child. He talked about making plans to visit soon and asked his mom about Sara. She told him that she talked to her every now and then, but that she didn't have her phone number because Sara didn't want her to, and she was okay with that.

Naomi and Essie were surprised because Sarah had never mentioned that she talked to Sara. Once they hung up with Andon, Naomi asked, "So you've been in contact with Sara?" "Yes," Sarah said. "She calls every now and then. I tell you that girl is just as evil as the day is dark. Whenever I talk to her, I end up feeling badly, like I have done something wrong. Given the way she talks to me, I wonder why she ever calls at all." "We were just talking about her the other day." "Well, she's fine, and that is all y'all need to know," Sarah said.

Life returned to normal for the Lavenders. Essie was working and going to school. Her brother was focusing on his girlfriend. Naomi was ready to have the baby. She stayed at Sarah's house because she needed more help now that she was getting closer to delivery. She planned to spend the first couple of months with her family so that she could get all the help she needed. Sarah was still working for the Montgomerys. She had become indispensable in the household. They all loved Miss Sarah, and she was making more money and had become a part of their family. They had given her a check for Naomi and the baby, and they bought a lot of baby items and were so excited that Sarah was about to be a grandmother.

One night, after they had eaten dinner, their father walked in. Essie jumped into his arms. Naomi was excited to see him too, but she couldn't move as quickly because she was huge. Sarah looked like she had seen a ghost. "How are you doing, Sarah?" he asked. "I'm well," she said with an attitude. Then they sat around the table, catching up. He had gotten a little heavier since the last time they saw him. He was no longer working at the Mill, but he had a decent job. He told Essie that he saw Jeanie a lot and asked if they were still friends. "Yes, we're still friends, but I barely see her now with work and school and all. "You know she's pregnant again?" he said. Essie shook her head no. "I ran into her the other day, and she told me she was five months. Essie said, "I need to go see her. She's probably mad at me. I haven't seen her or my godson in so long. We haven't spoken in a while either. I'm going to stop by sometime soon." "I'm sure she'll be happy to see you." Essie smiled and said, "I sure hope so."

"So, Dad," Naomi said, "How is Charlotte?" Andon looked surprised. He had assumed that they didn't care to know about her. Before he could say anything, Sarah said, "She's dead." He looked at Sarah and yelled, "How do you know that, Sarah? How do you know that?" Sarah looked frightened and started to stutter. Essie and Naomi looked confused. Andontis came out holding the telephone. Andon started yelling at Sarah. "You did that, Sarah? I can't believe you! You're evil!" He was crying and slobbering, looking like a crazy man. "I didn't do anything!" Sarah yelled back. "You did, Sarah. I knew it. I knew it! I can't believe you, Sarah. You're going to pay for what you did! I hate your guts—I swear I do. You're going to pay for this one. As God is my witness, Sarah Mae Lavender, you're going to pay!" He got up and left.

Now all the attention was focused on Sarah. Everyone looked at her for answers. "What is he talking about, Ma?" Essie asked. "I have no idea. He must be on drugs. Y'all see how big he got?" Sarah said, trying to throw them off. Naomi stared at her because what she was saying didn't make sense. "So how did you know she was dead?" Naomi asked. "Well, I don't know," Sarah said nervously. "I heard it somewhere." "Where did you hear it?" Naomi asked. "I don't know. I forgot," Sarah said, shrugging her shoulders. Essie got up from the table and went back to finish her homework. Andontis went back to his conversation on the phone. Sarah and Naomi were left at the table. Naomi sat staring at her mother, but Sarah avoided eye contact. She got up and started washing the dishes.

CHAPTER
TWELVE

ONE WEEK later, Essie went to Jeanie's after class. She still had a key, so she let herself in. Jeanie's son was sleeping on the couch. Essie called Jeanie's name, but no one answered, so she sat there hoping that Jeanie would return soon. A few minutes passed and Jeanie came in the door with two friends. Essie recognized one of them. "Hey," Essie said as they came in and noticed her sitting there. "What are you doing here?" Jeanie said. "I was just coming by to check on y'all since we haven't talked in a while." The girl that Essie recognized stared at her like she didn't like her. The other girl asked her who Essie was, glaring at her from head to toe as if she was an imposter. Before Jeanie answered, the other girl said, "That's Essie." Essie felt the tension so she asked Jeanie if they could speak in the other room. When they got to the bedroom, Essie asked Jeanie what was going on. "Did I do something to you?" Jeanie laughed sarcastically. "Did you do something? No, you ain't done a thing, Essie. That's exactly what you did…nothing!" "I don't understand," Essie said. "You think you're too good for little old me," Jeanie said. "You are supposed to be my baby's godmother, and we ain't seen you. He doesn't even know you. You haven't been here for us. You claim you care about us? Yeah right. You don't do anything for us. You think because you have a job and go to school that you are better than me. But you're not better than me, Essie. Not by a long shot. All that stuff you do doesn't make us different. You try to hide the real you behind that stuff, but we're one and the same. I ain't got no daddy. My baby don't got a daddy, and your daddy left y'all to be with a project chick. We don't know where my momma is, and y'all don't know where your sister is. She left y'all too. Naomi is slow as all outdoors, and your mama is crazy as hell, but you think you're better than me. Essie, you ain't better than me. You're just like me. Trying to act like you didn't want to stay in the projects…you *belong* here, Essie." Essie stood there with tears in her eyes, then realized that she didn't have to stand there and listen, so she walked out the front door. But Jeanie wasn't finished. She ran after her, yelling, screaming, and continuing to insult her. Essie was embarrassed and heartbroken and told herself that she would never talk to Jeanie again.

Essie went home, feeling down and sad about what had happened. Sarah asked her if she was okay. "Yes, I'm okay, Mama." "Your boss called and wanted to know if you could work tonight." Essie headed to work. She didn't even call to confirm that Mr. Melvin still needed her. She needed a break, and she didn't want to be at home so going to work was the outlet she needed.

"Hey, Essie. Thanks so much for coming in. I need to leave. My daughter is having my first grandbaby, and I want to be there. I appreciate you so much, my dear," said Mr. Melvin. "That's great, Mr. Melvin. Congratulations to you and the family," Essie said. Mr. Melvin was a spiritual man. A man of faith. He felt Essie's downtrodden spirit, and he stopped to ask if she was alright. Essie shrugged and said, "Yeah. I'm fine." "I'm sensing something coming from you, Essie. You know you can talk to me." Essie just stood there quietly. He walked over and hugged her tightly, and she began to weep in his arms. "It's okay, baby. Just let it all out." Essie cried like she had never cried before. She was hurt by what Jeanie had said, but she was also crying over how her life was going. She was dissatisfied. She missed her father. She hated her mother for pushing him away. She was sad for Naomi. She missed her sister Sara and didn't understand why she wasn't around. She missed Andon and was overwhelmed with the secret that she carried. The secret she kept hidden inside. The one that came to mind every time she thought of him. She was heartbroken for her family and wished she could just go back to the time when everything was normal.

After Essie's breakdown, Mr. Melvin asked her if she knew God. "Not really," she said. "I've heard of Him, but my family isn't religious. "Baby, knowing God isn't a religion. It's a relationship. I promise, knowing Him is the best thing to ever know. He cares for you; and even if you don't know Him, He knows you. He loves you and is concerned with everything that you're concerned with. God said that you are the apple of His eye. All you must do is welcome Him in. He is waiting for your invitation." "How do I do that?" Essie asked. "Just say this: 'Lord Jesus, please forgive me of my sins. I want to know you, Lord. I'm not perfect, but you were made perfect, so I don't have to be. I give you my heart. I give you my mind. I give you my soul, Lord. Come into my life. I welcome you into my life. You are welcome here, Lord. You are mine, and I am yours. You are now my personal Lord and Savior. Thank you, Jesus.'"

Once Essie had prayed the prayer, she felt a small sense of hope. She couldn't explain it, but she now felt safe. She felt a sense of peace and calm wash over her. Mr. Melvin felt her spirit shift, and he knew that she'd be alright. He said to her "Do not fret, my dear. Your help is here." She didn't understand, but she felt an urge to get to know the Jesus that Mr. Melvin spoke of. Essie felt peace all through the day. She felt the pain and worry melt away. She didn't even care about what Jeanie had said. She felt sorry for her, knowing that the pain she was trying to cause her was the pain she was carrying herself. Essie understood that what Jeanie said had nothing to do with her. She was projecting what she felt on Essie. "I am different than you, Jeanie," Essie thought to herself. Mr. Melvin had left with her the Lord's Prayer and told Essie to say it every morning when she woke up and every evening before bed.

When Essie got home later that night, the house was dark, and it felt peaceful. She peeked in her room to see if Naomi was there, but she wasn't. She knocked on Sarah's door and asked her where Naomi had gone. "Oh, she went home to get a few things. She said she needed some air, so she wanted a few minutes to herself. She should be back in a few. How are you doing, baby?" she asked Essie. "I'm good, Ma. How are you?" "I'm good too. Are you hungry? I left you some food on the stove." Essie ate, changed into her night clothes, and read the Lord's Prayer before falling asleep.

Naomi grabbed an overnight bag and started packing things for her and the baby. She felt like the baby was coming soon, and she wanted to be sure she had all she needed. She had all she could ever imagine needing. The Montgomerys had given Sarah so many things for the baby that she didn't have to buy anything else. They had even given her some baby books. As she was getting ready to leave, she heard something fall in her bedroom. It frightened her, and she started to head out the door, then stopped in her tracks thinking that it might be Sebastian coming back to her. "Sebastian?" she called out. Then a man appeared out of nowhere. Naomi wondered why he was in her apartment and how he got in. She knew he was White because of the blue eyes that pierced through the dark mask he had on. She tried to leave, but another man was behind her. He hit her in the back of the head with something, and she felt something in her head crush. She cried out in pain, and the man in front of her pushed her down. She tried to fight, but they were too strong. They pulled her by the legs, and Naomi tried to protect the baby by covering her stomach, but they continued to punch her. They stomped on her and kicked her stomach.

Naomi couldn't fight any more. She gave up, and they continued to beat her. Naomi's neighbor was awakened from her sleep and heard the noise coming from Naomi's apartment. She got up from her bed and looked out the peephole, then noticed two men leaving. One of the men looked at her door like he knew she was standing behind it. She jumped away from the peephole and stood to the side of the door. The men kept going. She waited for about fifteen minutes; then once she felt it was safe, she opened her door slowly and quietly and looked out to make sure they were gone. Naomi's door was open. She went back in her apartment to grab something to protect herself. The first thing she saw was her broom, so she grabbed it, then knocked on Naomi's door. "Naomi!" she called. "Naomi, are you in there?" She didn't hear anything, so she went in, peeking behind the door. She crept in slowly and noticed Naomi's bag on the floor close to the door. She called out again, "Naomi!" Still no answer. She proceeded to the bedroom and that's when she saw her. Naomi was laying there in a pool of blood. She went to her. "Oh my Lord, Naomi!" she cried. "Wake up, baby. Please wake up." Naomi was unrecognizable. They had beaten her badly, and there was blood everywhere. Blood was coming from her head, both of her eyes were swollen shut, and her lips and nose were bleeding and swollen. She had blood all over her clothes. She was in horrible shape. The neighbor picked up Naomi's phone, but it didn't work. She ran to her apartment as quickly as she could and called the police.

Essie heard her mother screaming her name. She got out of her bed and asked, "What's going on?" "We have to go! Naomi's in the hospital!" "She's in labor?" Essie asked, but Sarah didn't say anything. They headed to the hospital.

Essie, Sarah, and Andontis were in the waiting room. Sarah was crying uncontrollably. She felt responsible. Even though she didn't hurt Naomi herself, she felt like she caused it. She wanted to die. Essie watched her, wondering if her mother knew what happened to Naomi and why. She was angry, and she thought about what Mr. Melvin had just taught her. She couldn't help but think that maybe it had something to do with Naomi getting hurt. She used a payphone to call her dad; and when he answered, she explained to him that Naomi was hurt and asked him to come to the hospital. While Essie held the phone, tears welled up in her eyes. Sarah noticed it and hoped that he didn't tell her.

Essie was about to sit back down when the doctor came out calling their last name. "Can you follow me? She is in bad shape. She suffered blunt force trauma to her head. There are two gaping holes within inches of each other. We were able to stop the bleeding and stitch them up. It appears that someone may have hit her in the head twice. Her ribs are fractured, and her nose is broken. We're going to keep her here for a few days. We want to make sure that she and her baby are okay." "Can we see her?" Essie asked. "Yes, but let me warn you, she doesn't look like herself. Someone really did a number on her. It looks like someone beat her and tried to make her lose the baby. The baby is fine though. That little heart kept beating and wouldn't give up. We think the baby might've saved Naomi's life. I'm almost certain the baby will be fine."

They walked into Naomi's room. There were tubes and cords everywhere. The doctor was right; it didn't look like Naomi at all. They all cried, even Andontis. Sarah took it the hardest. She left the room, and they could hear her crying outside. The doctors tried to calm her down. Essie sat next to Naomi and just sobbed. Andontis hugged Essie as she cried. Essie began to pray, saying, "God, please save my sister and her baby", over and over. "Naomi, I need you to get up. We have a baby to take care of. You can't leave us, Nawni. You can't. We need you."

Sarah was outside in the hallway. She kept saying, "I'm sorry. I'm sorry. You can take me. Please not her. Not her. I'm sorry. I'm so sorry." A nurse took Sarah to an empty room. "Calm down, ma'am. Can I get you some water?" Sarah cried and couldn't stop. "There will be consequences. All firstborn boys will die." Sarah heard it in her head over and over. Then Sarah knew that Naomi's baby would die. She wanted to kill herself. She felt that if she was gone, then her children and grandchildren could be saved. She got up and left the hospital. As she was leaving, the machines in Naomi's room begin to go off. The nurse came in and raised the sheets, and there was blood on Naomi's hospital gown. Her water had burst. "Okay, we need you guys out," she said to Essie and Andontis, "She's in labor." Essie left the room looking for her mother to let her know the baby was coming but couldn't find her anywhere. They waited in the same room where the nurse took Sarah to calm down.

When Sarah got home, she was determined to end the curse that she and her ancestors had placed on her family. She spoke out loud. "You helped me destroy my family. Why is this happening? You helped me destroy my family." She knew that the only way to break this curse was for her to be burned to death. She looked in the kitchen cabinets for something to ignite a flame…and then an old woman appeared out of nowhere. She was very beautiful, and Sarah looked just like her. She had long, gray hair that looked like silk. She stood with her hands folded as she talked. "Sarah, you can't do this now. We all knew what would happen if this continued. You could have stopped this, but you kept going, Child. Now you got to live with what you've done. I'm sorry. This is the only way." Sarah sobbed. "Sarah, you can't burn your house. Where will the family go if you do this? This one wasn't on you. This is what I was sent to tell you. This one had nothing to do with us, Sarah? Go back to the hospital now." "No, no, no. I can't. I have to do this," Sarah said. "Answer the phone, Child," the old woman responded. "But it's not ringing," Sarah said. Then it rang.

"Hello? Mama? Naomi is about to have the baby." Sarah looked back, but the old woman was gone. "Hello, Mama? Are you there?" Sarah hung up the phone without saying anything. She left the house and headed back to the hospital.

Sarah got back to the hospital and Essie told her that Naomi was having a C-section. Sarah was a mess. Her eyes were puffy, and she looked disheveled. She was riddled with guilt. "The baby is going to die, Essie." Essie looked at her and said, "What do you mean the baby is going to die? How do you know that? The doctor said the baby is fine." Sarah kept shaking her head saying, "No, he is not fine. He is going to die." "He? We don't even know if it's a boy," Essie said. "Why would you say this? Have you lost your mind? Who are you? Get out! Get out!" Sarah stood there sobbing. Andontis went to her and put his hands on her shoulders. This startled Sarah, and she jumped back and looked at him like he was a stranger. "It's me, Mama," he said. She grabbed him and hugged him and whispered, "You won't be with us too much longer. I'm sorry." He pushed her away. "What is wrong with you?" Then he went to find Essie.

Hours later, they were all sitting in the waiting area when the doctor came in. Essie and her brother jumped up from where they were seated but Sarah didn't budge. "Congratulations. Naomi gave birth to a baby girl." Sarah turned and looked at the doctor in disbelief. "A girl?" she said. "Yes, a girl." Essie and her brother hugged, and Sarah cried out, saying "Thank you!" as she started to sob again.

"She is underweight. Naomi wasn't due for another couple of weeks so we're going to keep the baby and Naomi in ICU until they're both well enough to be released. We don't know how long that will be." "Can we see her?" Essie asked. "Yes. My nurse is cleaning her up. She has to be incubated at this time so as soon as she's ready, we will come back to get you all." "And Naomi?" Sarah asked. "Naomi has a long road ahead of her. We can't tell if the injuries she sustained will have a lasting effect. She took a brutal beating. She might be able to go home before the baby, but time will tell," said the doctor. "I'll have my nurse to come get you when the baby is ready."

They all sat quietly. Essie got up and went to her mother. "I'm sorry for yelling at you earlier, Mama." She hugged Sarah, and they cried together. Andontis followed, and they all cried. Essie silently thanked God for what He had done. Sarah still felt guilty about all that had happened, and she planned to tell Essie everything when they got home.

They were finally able to go in and meet Naomi's baby girl. She was so small. They couldn't tell who she would look like, but they could tell that her father was a White man. Her skin was so pale, and she had so much hair. Essie cried as she looked down at her niece in the incubator with tubes everywhere. She made a promise that she would love her like she was her own. Sarah wanted to reach in and grab her, but the doctors had instructed them not to touch her because she was so small. Essie and Sarah stood holding hands. Naomi's baby had brought them closer in an instant. Andontis stood there, looking at the baby; he too loved her. While he was staring at her, tears began to fall from his eyes. Sarah and Essie went in to see Naomi who was still unconscious. She wasn't aware of their presence—she wasn't even aware that she had given birth. The doctors told them that it would be a while before either of them could go home, as it would take some time for Naomi to recover.

When they got home later that evening, they talked about changing the house around to support Naomi and the baby. Andontis suggested that Naomi take the attic since it was bigger and would have enough room for her and all the baby's things. They all agreed, then Essie wondered whether Naomi would be able to carry the baby up and down the stairs. "You're right, Essie. Why don't we set up our room for Naomi and the baby? It's big enough for a crib and a bed for Naomi, and I will sleep in the front room. That way we'll both be close enough to help her." "Yes. Let's do that," Sarah said. "You could share the attic with me, Essie," her little brother said. "No way! I wouldn't be caught dead in the attic. Thanks, but no thanks!" They all laughed.

The atmosphere in the house was calm. Essie and Sarah had bathed and put on pajamas. Andontis was in Sarah's room on the phone with his girlfriend. Essie was in her bedroom going over all that had happened when Sarah had come in and asked her if they could talk. She jumped up and said, "Sure, Mama. What's up?" "I want to talk to you about something. I just want you to be aware of what this thing is."

Sarah thought she should tell Essie because someone else other than her needed to know and understand the curse. She knew Essie was the strongest of her daughters, even though she was the youngest. She knew she could handle it…and she was the only one there. She made them a small meal and began to tell her what her grandmother had told her about how the curse started and where it originated from. As Sarah was telling her the story, Essie thought back to the time her friend had said her mother was a witch. "My mama said all y'all witches, and she don't want me playing with you." Now it was all starting to make sense. "So, your mother, Sarah, started all this?" Essie asked. "It didn't start with her. It started with her mother, my grandmother Sarah, but my mother kept it going for years. She used what she learned to her advantage." "So, the same Montgomerys who had your family as slaves are the ones you work for now?" "Well, yes…in a sense. None of them are alive now, but their family still lives in that house." "Do they know your family were slaves there?" "I believe they do which is why they let me work there."

"Was your father a slave too?" "No. My father was a Montgomery." Essie sat there with her mouth open. "Oh my God. So, my grandfather was a White man? Did he know you were his child?" "Yes." "Did you meet him?" "No, not really." "So how do you know?" Essie asked.

"My mother died when I was thirteen. On her death bed, she explained all of this to me. She gave me their address, and I used to go by there just to see what the place looked like. I never got close enough to go in; until one day, I saw an ad for a housemaid at the Montgomery Plantation. I inquired, and they hired me on the spot. I started working the same day I showed up.

Over the years, I was able to confirm the things my mother had told me about them. I believe my father was still alive when I started working there. He was ill, and they kept him in a room where I wasn't allowed. One night, he got really sick, and they had to take him to the hospital. On his way out, I made sure to get a glimpse of him. He was in a wheelchair. He stared at me, and we had the same eyes. I felt like it was him, but I didn't know for sure. A couple of weeks after that, he was home and back in the room where they kept him. He had a nurse with him twenty-four hours a day. One day, as I was cleaning near the room, the nurse had stepped out, so I went in to get a closer look. He was awake and sitting up in his bed. He couldn't talk; but when I got inside the room, I just stood there looking at him and he looked at me too. He looked like he was happy to see me, but I couldn't tell if he was or not. He stretched out his hand as if he wanted me to come closer. Before I could get to him, the nurse came back and put me out of the room, and I never got that opportunity again." "Wow, Ma. I can't imagine living in a world without a mother or a father," Essie said. "Well, my MawMaw lived long after my mother did. She didn't want me working at the Montgomery's—she despised them. She hated them with a passion. I learned all I know from her. She wanted to "equip" me, she used to say— she wanted me to be armed, just in case the Montgomerys tried me." Sarah giggled a bit to herself. "She was a strong woman though. She had gone through a lot in her life, from being a slave to being a widow, and then having to raise me after my mama died. She didn't take no mess from no one. Through her, I always felt empowered. You know? Like I could take over the world. I looked a lot like MawMaw. My mother and I were named after her." Essie knew this because her mother always talked about her MawMaw and why she named her first daughter after her. "But she had some secrets. Secrets of a deep and dark past. She told me about it all. She told me my mother stayed at the plantation where my ancestors were slaves for a long time after they were freed. While she was there, she didn't visit the family. In fact, MawMaw said she'd disowned them. Until she got pregnant with me. MawMaw said she came home when she was about eight months pregnant because she was too big to fulfill her obligations to Mr. Montgomery, and he was no longer attracted to her. And he knew she couldn't give birth to me there because it would tarnish the Montgomery's reputation. His family all knew that he was having sex with my mother. They knew he was in love with her. They also knew I was his child. But they couldn't have the slave girl staying and working there carrying a Montgomery baby."

Back then...

It was late, and the entire house was quiet. It was pouring rain and thundering outside. There was a quiet knock on the door. Sarah (MawMaw) was sitting in her chair, reading the special recipes that were passed down to her from her ancestors. It was a book filled with spells, maps, Bible verses, and names of those who had come before her. She ignored the knock, thinking it was just the wind from the storm. The knock got louder. Sarah got up and grabbed her shotgun as she eased toward her door, and the knock grew louder and louder. She peeped out of the window and saw her daughter standing there. Pregnant. She put her gun down and opened the door. Her daughter was standing there, crying. Sarah embraced her while she cried. "He kicked me out, Mama. He doesn't want me or the baby. He said it wasn't his. He said he couldn't embarrass his family name by having a baby with a nigger. He never talked to me like that before." Sarah didn't say anything. She held her baby in her arms and let her cry. She wasn't mad at her—she knew this day would come. She'd also planned to make sure he paid for treating her daughter that way. But she had to wait until the baby was born. She needed something of his and with her child carrying his child, she would have a piece of his flesh.

Back at the kitchen table...

Essie just sat there, taking it all in. It was almost as if she understood her mother. She wanted to ask her about the spells and if she was really a witch. But she just sat there, listening to every word her mother spoke. She wanted to know more, and she didn't want to move from the table. She felt like it was story time.

"So, what did she do?" Essie asked. "Well, I'm not exactly sure what it was she did. But I do know she took care of him," Sarah said. "How did she take care of them?" Essie asked. "She cast a spell on him." Essie looked shocked. "What do you mean she cast a spell?" Sarah took a long, deep breath. "All I know is that she waited until I was born to complete it." "She didn't tell you what she did or how she did it?" Essie asked. "No, she didn't; but as I got older, I understood because she taught me how to do it." "Do you think she is the reason your father...I mean the man you believed was your father...do you think she made him sick?" "Possibly," Sarah said. Andontis came out of the bedroom and headed to the attic, interrupting their conversation.

Sarah said that it was getting late, but Essie didn't want the time to end. "I'm not tired," she said. "Are you tired?" "Yes, baby. To be honest, I am exhausted. But don't worry. I promise, I will tell you everything. I won't leave anything out, even though some of it might upset you. But I promise you will know everything, okay?" They hugged and then went to bed.

A week later...

Essie and Mr. Melvin were preparing to close the store for the evening, and he asked how Naomi was doing. "She is doing better physically but..." Essie paused. "What?" Mr. Melvin asked. "I feel like her mind isn't all the way there, you know?" "Sometimes, it takes time for everything to get back to normal," said Mr. Melvin. Essie shrugged and said, "I guess. We have never had anything like this happen in our family, and we're all kind of freaked out." "Don't worry, baby. It is all in God's control. We've been praying for you all, and I got the church to add you all to our weekly prayer list." "Thank you so much, Mr. Melvin. I really appreciate it."

On the walk home, Essie spotted her brother walking with a young lady. It appeared that they were on their way to the Lavender's house. Essie walked behind them, observing their interaction. Andontis looked excited. He talked and talked. He had his arm around her at first and then he grabbed her hand. They walked and held hands for a second, then she appeared uncomfortable with the affection and pulled her hand away. Essie quickened her steps, trying to get close enough to hear their conversation without being noticed. Essie had a strange feeling about the girl. Watching her body language, she felt like something was off. As Essie got closer, she heard Andontis say "Don't worry. It will be fine, I promise. My family is cool. They already know about you." "What do you mean they know about me?" the girl asked. "I mean, we talk on the phone all the time. They know I'm talking to my girlfriend," he said.

Before they got to the house, the girl turned down the alleyway next to the Barn, and Andontis followed. Essie got close enough to hear the girl yelling. "I told you, I wasn't comfortable with all of this!" "All of what?" he said. "It wasn't supposed to get to this," she said. "Shelly, I am so confused right now. One minute, you act like you love me and want to be with me; and then the next, you act as if you don't want any part of this. Just tell me what you want." Shelly was crying, and she yelled at him and said, "I don't know what I want. I'm not ready for this!" "Ready for what?" Andontis yelled back. "I never dated a nig…I never dated a colored boy before. And I know my family will be against it. I am not sure if we should continue like this." Andontis looked disappointed. "You told me you wanted this. You said I was different, and that's why you liked me so much." "I know but, I didn't think it would go as far as you wanting me to meet your family. No one was supposed to know about this. We agreed to keep it a secret. It was better that way."

Essie came around the corner and interrupted their conversation, purposely intruding because she heard what the girl said to her baby brother. "Hello," she said. "I'm Essie, Andontis' older sister." She extended her hand to the girl, a White girl with red hair, green eyes, and freckles. Shelly looked startled. She looked at Andontis then back at Essie, who still had her hand out waiting for her to accept the offer. Although Essie knew she wouldn't, she continued with the "fake" gesture of kindness. Shelly walked off without saying anything to either of them, and Andontis followed her, calling her name. Shelly began to run, and he chased her for a while; but then gave up and walked back over to Essie. "What's the deal, Essie?" he said angrily. "Why did you do that?" "Do what?" Essie said. "All I wanted to do was introduce myself. That can't possibly be the girl you've been talking to every day. Because at least that girl seems to like you. But this one? This one is totally ashamed of you. I bet her family is a bunch of racists. She doesn't even want to be seen with you. Why would you want somebody like that? You deserve better than that, Dontis." "Well, her brother is the captain of our team. She doesn't want him to know." "Why not? You are teammates, right?" "Yeah, but he wouldn't want me dating his little sister. But we talked about this over a week ago. We talked about letting both of our families know. She said she was going to talk to Barry, and we were going to introduce each other to our families. Now she's acting as if the conversation never happened. It's like she's a whole different person on the phone." "Well maybe, you should just give it a rest then. Give her some time to think about what she wants," Essie said. They walked around the neighborhood for about an hour before walking the rest of the way home.

When they got to the door, Andontis grabbed Essie's arm. "Please don't mention any of this to Mama." "Why not?" Essie asked. "Because" he said. "Because what?" "Essie, you know," he said. "I know what?" Essie said. "I don't want anything to happen to Shelly," he pleaded. "What?" Essie said with a smirk. "Why would anything happen to her?" "Essie, you know," he said again, looking embarrassed. Then he grew closer to her and said under his breath, "I don't want Mama to kill her." This shocked Essie, and she wondered where he had heard this.

Andontis pushed past Essie and went into the house, and she stood there processing what her brother had said. When Essie finally went into the house, she heard the telephone ring and heard Sarah call Andontis. "Who is it?" he asked. "Who else?" she said, handing him the phone. He noticed Essie standing there, and they locked eyes for a second, then he walked into his mother's bedroom. "Hey, baby," Shelly said. "Hey," he responded. He wasn't surprised as this had become her normal behavior. "What's going on, Shelly?" He asked. "What do you mean?" "Well, we can't pretend that what just happened didn't happen." Shelly chuckled and said, "Whatever do you mean? We had a wonderful time together." Before Andontis could reply, he heard Shelly talking to her father, and she hung up the phone without saying goodbye.

Shelly's residence...

Shelly heard her father calling her name from the dining room. "Yes, Papa?" she answered. "Get down here. It's time for dinner." As Shelly entered the dining room, she watched the maid pour her mother some iced tea. Barry was already sitting at the table. Her mother, who was "ill," sat at the table, still in her night clothes, looking disheveled. She didn't say anything. She looked up at the maid and smiled as she set the jug of iced tea in the center of the table. Shelly, who for an instant had appeared to be happy and in a good mood suddenly became sad and quiet as she sat down. Her father said grace. When he finished, he picked up his fork and began to eat. Barry started eating, and their mother looked around the table, smiling at everyone. "What's wrong, Shelly? Eat your food," her father said. Shelly stared at her plate. "I'm not hungry, Papa," she said. "Shelly, eat. We're not going to have this nonsense. Mabel prepared this lovely dinner for us, and it's not going to waste. Now eat," he demanded. Shelly began to cry and said, "I don't want it." Then suddenly, their mother pushed her plate to the floor, breaking it. "No!" she yelled over and over. Mabel and the nurse ran into the kitchen. They grabbed her and began to console her as they led her back to the bedroom. "You see what you did?" Shelly's father said. You upset your mother." He wiped his mouth, and threw his napkin on the table, then stormed out.

Later that evening, Shelly was in her bedroom, exhausted from crying. Barry came in and sat on the edge of her bed. "What's wrong with me?" she asked him. He grabbed her and hugged her, rubbing her head. "Nothing's wrong with you, Shelly. You're perfect." He loved his baby sister so much, but he knew that it was only a matter of time before she succumbed to the same illness as their mother. He cried silently so that Shelly did not notice.

CHAPTER
THIRTEEN

TWO months had passed since the birth of Naomi's baby girl. She had needed help walking for a while but had made progress in the past three weeks. The baby was doing well. The doctors could not tell if she would have any developmental delays, but they wanted to monitor her closely and had scheduled weekly checkups.

Naomi was in a deep depression. She didn't want to hold or nurse her baby. Her doctor tried to get her to bond with the baby, but Naomi refused. Essie and Sarah spent a lot of time at the hospital. They were totally smitten with the baby and loved her so much. They too tried to get Naomi to engage with her daughter, but to no avail. The nurse would bring the baby in her room at the same time each day, but Naomi wouldn't even look at her. In the two months since the baby was born, she had never even held her. She hadn't even named her. Naomi was overwhelmed with the guilt of not wanting her own child, the very flesh of her flesh and bone of her bone. The shame of how she was conceived— out of lust and infatuation and not of love—overwhelmed her. Naomi was reminded how she could have lost her and secretly wished that she would have. She was Sebastian's child, and Naomi hated that part of her.

It was time for Naomi and her daughter to be released from the hospital, and Sarah and Essie were so excited that they were coming home. They had prepared the house for the baby and rearranged their schedule so at least one of them would always be home to help Naomi. Naomi's doctor had provided specific instructions for her and the baby's home-care, and she also gave Sarah the follow-up doctor's appointment schedule. The doctor also sent home a full box of formula to feed the baby, since Naomi had not nursed her. Since they didn't have a car, the doctor ordered a small medical bus to transport them all home. Sarah held her new granddaughter in her arms, smiling and talking baby talk to her while Essie sat next to Naomi, holding her hand. Naomi didn't speak a word but rested her head on Essie's shoulder the entire ride home.

When the Lavenders arrived home, it seemed as if the entire neighborhood was there waiting for them, crowded in front of the house. They had gifts for Naomi and her baby girl. They all knew what had happened and wanted to show their support for them. They cheered and congratulated them as they exited the van, and Sarah smiled with pride. She showed the baby off to everyone that asked to see her, and everyone gushed over how beautiful she was. Essie pushed past them, taking Naomi into the house. The neighbors asked Sarah for the baby's name, but she ignored them.

When Naomi and Essie got into the house, Naomi noticed how much it had changed. The bedroom had been redecorated and there was a bassinet next to her bed. Pastel colors filled the space; teddy bears and small trinkets were everywhere. Naomi stood there for a second, looking at it all and feeling detached and numb. Then tears filled her eyes. Essie hugged her and promised her that everything would be okay.

In the first couple of weeks, everyone in the household adjusted to Naomi being home. Sarah was there the whole time. She took extra time off from work because she didn't want to leave her granddaughter's side, and she wasn't comfortable leaving Naomi alone with her. Essie continued to work and started her second year of college. Mr. Melvin had increased her pay and given her more responsibilities around the store. She hired two more employees and paid Andontis to sweep up and mop the store occasionally. Essie basically ran the store. She did everything; ordering, inventory, payroll, training the new hires, and setting their schedules. Mr. Melvin loved Essie like a daughter and trusted her, so much so that he rarely had to be there. Essie was in the business management program at school and was gaining the knowledge that she needed to run the store. She even taught Mr. Melvin some things about business, and he was open to all the insight that she offered. He knew she was a gem, and he was thankful for her. As a result, the store was doing well.

One evening, Essie was getting ready to close. She had completed the inventory for the day and was just about to put the "We're closed. See ya tomorrow." sign in the window when a young girl walked in. Essie was about to tell her they were closed but then stopped. "Can I help you with something?" she asked. The girl ignored Essie and continued walking to the back of the store. "I'm about to close up so if you could grab what you need quickly, that would be greatly appreciated." The girl didn't say anything but continued to shop. Essie went back to open the cash register so she could check the girl out; but after about ten minutes, she walked swiftly past Essie and attempted to leave the store. Essie yelled, "Excuse me! Are you going to pay for that?" The girl continued to the door; but when she pulled the handle to open it, she realized that it was locked. She panicked, looking for a way to unlock it. Essie stood there, watching the girl becoming annoyed. "You can't leave without paying for your groceries." Finally, the girl realized that she couldn't get out and started to cry. Essie stood there with her arms folded and stared at her. The girl started crying hysterically and slid to the floor sobbing. Essie softened and grabbed some paper towels off the counter, then handed them to the distraught girl.

The girl finally spoke. "I'm sorry. I don't have any money." "Why would you come to the store if you knew you didn't have any money?" The girl took a deep breath and said, "There's no food in the house. I haven't eaten anything since lunch at school today. I got desperate, I guess." "Where are your parents?" Essie asked. "My mom is at home," said the girl. Then Essie examined her.

Her shoes were worn, and the jacket she had on was filthy and at least three sizes too big. The pants she had on were too small. Her hair was pulled back in a neat ponytail with a shoestring to hold it in place. Essie grabbed a shopping bag and started to bag the groceries that the girl had grabbed. Then she helped her up off the floor. "Is this all you need?" Essie asked. The girl looked at her, not sure what to say. Essie then grabbed a second shopping bag and handed it to her. "Go ahead, and fill the bags up. Get what you need." "Are you sure?" the girl asked. "Yes. Go ahead, and take your time." Essie said. The girl went from aisle to aisle, filling the bags until there was no more room in them. Essie grabbed another shopping bag and started separating the things and placing them in the bag. "Thank you, and I'm so sorry." "Don't worry about it," Essie said. "What's your name?" "Essie. What's yours?" "My name is Josette, but everyone calls me JoJo." "Well, it's nice to meet you JoJo." "It's nice to meet you too Essie, and thank you again." Essie grabbed some hair ties from behind the counter and gave them to her. JoJo's eyes lit up, and she hugged Essie. "Where do you live?" Essie asked. "I stay on Markham Avenue near Taylor Street. It's just three blocks over." "Okay. I'll walk you home." "You don't have to," JoJo said. "I know, but I'd like to. Plus, you need help carrying all this stuff. Is that okay with you?" JoJo smiled and nodded.

When Essie got home, Sarah was rocking her granddaughter to sleep. She motioned for her to keep quiet, so she tiptoed past. Naomi was in the bedroom with all the lights turned out. Once Sarah got the baby to sleep, she took her into the room with Naomi and laid her in the bassinet. Essie was sitting at the kitchen table with her feet up, and her head resting on the back of the chair. She was exhausted, and all she wanted to do was lie down. Since Naomi and the baby came home, Essie's bed was in the living room on the couch. "Hey, sweetie. Are you okay?" Sarah asked. I'm fine. Just tired. You wouldn't believe the night I just had." Essie said.

Essie told Sarah all that had just happened with JoJo at the store. "I was wondering why you got home later than usual. You did a good thing today, baby," Sarah said, placing her hand on Essie's cheek and looking into her beautiful eyes. Essie felt that the gesture was a bit off, but she thanked her mother anyway. "Are you hungry? Let me fix you something to eat," Sarah said. "That's alright. I really just want to lie down, and get some rest," Essie said. "Okay, but before you do that, we need to talk. I need to get back to work. I've taken all the time I can. Do you think you can rearrange your work and school schedule so that one of us can be here with Naomi and the baby at all times?" "Yes. I don't see why not. I've already hired more help at the store so that shouldn't be a problem. When are you going back?" Essie asked. "They want me back two weeks from now." "Okay. That will be enough time for me to let Mr. Melvin know and adjust the schedules." Sarah thanked her, and Essie went to lie down. The minute she did, she fell asleep. Naomi overheard the conversation that Sarah and Essie were having. She felt horrible that they now had to adjust their schedules in order to help her with her baby. She felt like she needed to be babysat…and she didn't like that feeling at all. She got out of bed and walked over to the bassinet where her baby girl was sleeping. She wanted to see if she could feel something other than the pain of not wanting her. Thinking that if she could love her, she could start being a mother to her, and everything else could get back to normal. As she stared at her baby, the guilt and the shame hit her like a ton of bricks. She got back into bed and cried. She felt helpless and hopeless. She had accepted the fact that she would be having a baby the moment she found out that she was pregnant. She had made a choice then to love her baby unconditionally. However, the unforeseen circumstances that had come about pushed her to an unfortunate mental state. She wanted to love her child. She wanted to be the mother she had dreamed of being…but she just couldn't. It was too painful. But she knew it wasn't the baby's fault. She didn't choose to be born.

Naomi's Dream…

Naomi woke up and saw Sebastian standing over their baby. She knew it was him as he stood there with his back to her, looking down at their daughter in her bassinet. He picked her up and walked out of their bedroom and out the front door. Naomi called out his name, "Sebastian! Sebastian!" He didn't answer. He kept walking, never acknowledging her. As he walked out the door to his car, he stopped cradling the baby and started to drag her by her arm like she was a doll. The baby cried. As Naomi tried to get to him and her daughter, he threw the baby into the back seat of the car, got in, and drove off. Naomi yelled out, "No! Give me my baby!" Naomi chased the car but couldn't catch up. She was running in slow motion. She felt like something was holding her back, and she looked down at her feet. She was sinking in quicksand. She was trying to maintain her balance, but she continued to sink. Suddenly, an unseen force helped her out of the sinking sand. This force then handed her two pairs of shoes, pointed to the east and told her to put the shoes on and walk. Naomi put on a pair of the shoes and walked. Even though it seemed like she walked forever, she wasn't tired. The shoes she had on were comfortable and provided the endurance she needed to keep moving forward. Naomi then noticed a small cabin in her path. She walked to it and entered. "Hello?" She called as she closed the door behind her. In the house were two rooms. Naomi went into the first room where an elderly woman with long, flowing white hair was standing in the corner. "Hello?" Naomi said. "I'm looking for my baby. I have to give her these shoes." The woman didn't move, but Naomi could see that she was holding something. As Naomi walked closer, she realized it was her baby. Her eyes lit up. She was so happy to see her daughter. She had never felt the love she now felt for her baby. The woman turned towards Naomi and allowed her to put the shoes on her daughter's feet. Once the shoes were on her baby's feet, the elderly woman said to her, "She is yours." For the first time, Naomi noticed her daughter's eyes. They were a beautiful blue. She noticed that the lady eyes were also blue. "Thank you so much, ma'am," Naomi said. "I know she's mine. I love her so much." Naomi held her baby and cried. She said repeatedly, "I'm sorry, I'm sorry," as she held and kissed her daughter. "Naomi!" The lady called out to her. Naomi heard it, but she couldn't let her daughter go. "Naomi!" She heard her name again. Then she woke up to Essie standing over her.

When Naomi realized it was just a dream, she jumped out of bed and grabbed her daughter from her bassinet. Just as in the dream, Naomi held her daughter and cried saying, "I'm so sorry. I'm so sorry." Essie stood there watching, not understanding what was going on. She walked over to Naomi while she was holding her daughter and just stood next to her with her arm wrapped around her shoulder. Essie started to cry because she was happy that Naomi was now holding her daughter and loving her like she knew she could and eventually would.

Sarah then came into the room. She was startled to see Naomi holding the baby and was about to take the baby out of Naomi's arms, but Essie stopped her. Sarah walked closer and wrapped her arm around Naomi, and they all stood there crying. "What is her name?" Sarah asked Naomi. "Her name is Olivia," Naomi said. "Olivia Ester Lavender"

FOURTEEN

NINE months passed, and the Lavender home was more peaceful than it had ever been. Naomi had progressed and adjusted well. She walked with a slight limp, but only those who knew what had happened to her noticed it. Olivia, whose nickname was "Livi," had also blossomed into a bright-eyed, bushy-tailed baby girl that the entire family was obsessed with. Her doctors were surprised at her development as they had assumed that she would be delayed in some way; however, Livi was right on target. She was crawling and sitting up and had just started to stand on her own. She needed to be watched at all times because she got into everything. Naomi was a great mother. She read to her baby as often as she could. She sang to her and was teaching how to say "mama." "Da-da" was her first word, and Naomi was proud of her, but she hated that her baby said that word first.

Naomi had started tutoring again. She had eight clients in total—six White and two Black clients in the neighborhood. She was paid handsomely, and it gave her the opportunity to set her own hours and not have to spend much time away from Livi. Essie was still running the store which had expanded into a large grocery store built from the ground up. She was the manager of the store, still in charge of hiring, scheduling, training, and inventory. Andontis had just graduated from high school and was preparing to start college in the fall. Sarah still worked for the Montgomerys but only two nights a week. She kept Livi while Naomi worked.

"I think we should move and get a bigger home," Naomi said one night as they were eating dinner. "You think so?" Sarah asked. Essie didn't say anything because she was thinking about moving out on her own. She had even looked at a couple of apartments close to the store, but she wasn't going to tell her family until she got one. "What do you think, Essie?" Sarah asked. "I think it's a good idea," she said hesitantly. Sarah noticed her apprehension and took note of it. "We can sell this house and use the profit for a down payment on another," Naomi said. "Oh, this old house?" Sarah said. "I don't think anybody would want this." Essie and Naomi were confused.

"What's happening, everybody?" Andontis came in and grabbed Livi from her highchair, swinging her around, and lifting her in the air. "Hey, LiviLivi," he said, hugging and kissing her cheeks. Livi giggled.

"Are you hungry, baby?" Sarah asked him. "No. I'm heading out," he said. "Heading out? You just got in," Sarah said. Andontis handed Livi off to Essie. "I know, Ma. I'm going to hang out with Franny for the night." Essie asked him who Franny was, and he said that she was his girlfriend. "What ever happened to Shelly?" Essie asked. "She's still around, but I don't talk to her much. She's too confusing and moody. I can't ever tell what's up with her," Andontis said. "Well, she still calls here every day," Sarah said. "It's annoying. One night, she called at two in the morning. I told her you weren't here, and she got to questioning me. I had to hang up on her, and she continued to call back until I got up and unplugged the phone." "Really? That's crazy," Naomi said. Andontis sighed and shook his head as he headed to the attic to pack an overnight bag.

Naomi wasted no time at all when she found out they were all in agreement about moving. She had an appraiser come to their home the following week to let them know how much they could get for the house. As he walked around making notes on his clipboard, he showed no emotion. Naomi was looking for assurance that the house was worth selling. Essie and Andontis were not home, and Sarah and Livi were taking a nap. "How much did you pay for this house?" the appraiser asked Naomi. "I don't know. My parents bought it before I was born." "Oh, that explains it," he said. "What do you mean?" Naomi asked. "Well, there is a lot of wear and tear on this house, and it's very old. However, I do believe if you make some additions and repairs to the house, you could sell it for a decent penny. You can start with those backsteps," he said pointing to the backdoor in the kitchen. "You could easily make it a full porch or a deck. Also, making the backyard look like an actual backyard by adding flowers and some gardening there. And the appliances in this kitchen are so old. You will certainly need to update everything in here to make a sale. Now the bedrooms and the living room are in good shape, from what I can see. I think by adding some fresh paint to the walls, you will be good there. You can add another bedroom in the attic." He walked over to the huge window where Sara, her sister, used to sit when she lived there. He appeared to be fascinated by it. "This is a beauty. You can expand the walls outside of the borders here, and make this a balcony or a deck. This window is the most attractive thing about this house, respectfully. Of course, you'd have to repair all the windows in the house and repair the exterior."

Naomi was a little discouraged. "So really, this house isn't even worth selling without doing all those suggested repairs?" she asked. "Well, that is the key, Miss. These are all just suggestions. Whether you do them or not is up to you. But I honestly don't think you'll get much for this house if you don't." "Wow," Naomi said. "Thank you for your time."

Naomi paid him for his services, walked him to the door, and then sat down on the couch were Essie slept, pondering what she would do about the house. She was determined to move out with her family this time. She had grown closer to all of them after Livi was born. She gained a new love and respect for them all and felt like things would be better if they all lived together. Naomi feared being alone. She didn't have any memories of the attack in her home before Livi was born, but the thought of not having her family with her scared her, and that motivated her to keep looking. She decided not to give up on looking for a new place to live for her and her family, but she did give up on selling their house. After sitting there for a few minutes, she went to the kitchen to start dinner.

Essie had just gotten her last refund payment for the semester. She looked at the amount and then put it in her backpack as she left campus. On her way to work, she stopped at the bank. This was the same bank where she took the deposits from the store. It was the only bank in town that would allow her to open an account. All the other banks were owned by racist White folks that wouldn't allow the wealthiest Black person to even enter their bank, let alone use their banking services. Although slavery had died decades ago, racism was still very much alive.

As Essie got closer to the store, she noticed Andontis talking to Shelly. Shelly was crying, and it looked like Andontis was trying to reason with her. She got close enough to hear the conversation. "I'm not interested in you anymore, Shelly. You gotta get out of here," he said as he tried to get her to leave. "Why, Andontis? You said you would always love me," Shelly said. "I know, and I do, Shelly. I'm just not *in* love with you." Shelly slapped him, and Essie jumped between them before things escalated further. "Why would you do that?" she yelled at Shelly. Shelly turned from a distraught little girl to a pompous White woman. "Who are you? Get your nigger hands off me," she said to Essie. This surprised Essie, and she loosened her grip. "Excuse me?" Essie said. "You heard me," Shelly said. At this point, some of the customers from the store started to gather around. "Get out of here, you honky," one of them yelled at Shelly. "We don't need your kind around here," someone else said. Shelly gathered herself and looked at Andontis with the most hateful look. "Alright then. I will leave, but you know this isn't the end," she said as she walked away.

Just as Shelly was leaving, Franny walked up. Shelly turned around to watch as she walked over to Andontis. She then turned back into a distraught little girl and ran off crying. "What was that about?" Franny asked as she grabbed his hand. "I'll tell you about it later," he said. Essie was so upset; she didn't even acknowledge Franny. She stormed into the store to begin her shift.

Later that evening, Essie sat at the kitchen table with her mom and Naomi, telling them about the events of the day. "Something just rubs me the wrong way about the girl," Sarah said. "What do you think she meant by saying 'it's not the end?'" "I don't know," Essie said. "She was probably just saying that because she was angry." "No. I think she might be planning something," Sarah replied. Naomi said, "What could she possibly be planning?" "I don't know. But that statement just doesn't sit well with me."

Andontis didn't come home that night. Sarah tossed and turned the entire night, wondering if this would be the night the promise on Andontis' life would be fulfilled. She knew there wasn't anything that she could do to stop it, but she was hoping and praying for more time with him before his life would innocently be taken away because of the curse on their family. Then she heard something in the kitchen and jumped up to see if it was him. It was Essie, getting a glass of water. She looked at Sarah and knew something was bothering her. She asked Sarah if she was okay, and she took a deep breath and said, "No, I'm not alright." She sat down at the table, and Essie followed.

They sat at the table for hours as Sarah explained the generational curse that was on their bloodline. Essie cried because she didn't want to lose her baby brother. "Can we move him out of town or send him away?" she sobbed. "We can, but that won't stop it," Sarah said. She and Essie held one another and cried. "I wish I could take it back. After this thing with him and the White girl, I feel like the time is near." Essie got up and got another glass of water from the sink. "We have to do something, Mama. We have to." Then she said hopefully, "Nothing happened to Andon, so maybe nothing will happen to Andontis!" Sarah lowered her eyes.

"What?" Essie asked, seeing the look on Sarah's face. "If there is something you need to say, you might as well say it." "Andon isn't my son." Essie dropped the glass on the floor, shattering it. She asked Sarah what she meant, and she said, "He is your father's son, but not mine."

Sarah was seventeen years old and had been working on the Montgomery plantation for a couple of years. She took the bus every morning, and soon she noticed Andon Sr. He would get on the bus at the same spot every morning on his way to work. She thought he was very handsome, but he never noticed her. Sarah used to get herself all dolled up every morning, hoping that he would notice her. He never did, and one day, Sarah got up the courage to go sit next to him on the bus. "Hi," she said as she sat down next to him. "Hello," he said, then turned his attention back to the newspaper he was reading. "My name is Sarah," she said. "Okay," he replied, not looking up from his paper. "Well. When a girl introduces herself, she usually expects the same in return," she snapped. This got Andon's attention, and he looked up; and for the first time, he noticed her. He saw how beautiful she was, and how her eyes were tantalizing. "I'm Andon," he said, smiling at her. "Nice to meet you, Andon," Sarah said as she held out her hand.

From then on every morning, they shared a seat and talked, getting to know one another. He was from Haiti and had come to the United States to work at the Mill. The only time they saw each other was on the bus. Andon never asked Sarah out on a date or acted like he wanted to spend more time with her. After a couple of months, Sarah became impatient and made up her mind to ask him out.

One morning, as she was getting off the bus, she kissed him. He was shocked, but Sarah could tell that he liked it. The next day, she planned to ask if they could spend more time together, but he didn't get on the bus. Soon it had been four days since he had ridden the bus. Sarah was concerned, but she knew nothing about him other than he was from Haiti, and he worked at the Mill, but she didn't know where that was. She decided to find out, though. Sarah was very resourceful. She asked her MawMaw where the Mill was, but she didn't know either. She searched the newspapers to find out but still had no luck.

Sarah was determined to find out where the Mill was. She made herself sick with the thought of never seeing Andon again. She was in love with him. She had already made up in her mind that he was hers and that they would live together and have beautiful children.

There was a guy in Sarah's neighborhood who was infatuated with her. He bought her flowers and gifts, and her MawMaw just knew that he was the one for Sarah. She encouraged him to continue pursuing her, telling him that she would give in one day. But Sarah wasn't interested in him at all.

One night, Sarah was sitting on the stoop in front of MawMaw's house when Timmy walked up. "Hey, Sarah," he said and smiled at her. "Hey, Timmy," Sarah said. "Why are you looking all sad, gal? What's up with you?" She asked him if he had ever heard of the Mill, and he said that he had, then asked her what she knew about it. She ignored the question and asked him where it was.

Timmy asked her if she had business there. She shrugged, saying that she just wanted to know where it was. She pressed him, and he said that he knew where it was and that it was a way away. Sarah asked him to take her there, and he was confused, but he adored her and agreed. She jumped up, and he said, "We can't go right now. Let's go tomorrow afternoon when you get off work." She was annoyed at the delay, but she knew she didn't have any choice, so she agreed.

Sarah didn't get any sleep that night. She couldn't wait to get to the Mill to see Andon. She didn't even go to work the next day because she was getting herself prepared to see him. She picked out her best outfit and perfume. She was so excited. MawMaw knocked on her bedroom door and entered without waiting for her to answer. "Sarah, why didn't you go to work? Someone called from the Montgomery plantation asking why you aren't there," she said. "I don't feel well," Sarah said. MawMaw walked over to her to feel her head. "You don't have a fever." "I'm tired. I didn't feel like going today." Then MawMaw noticed Sarah's clothes laid out on the bed. She asked Sarah where she was going, and she told her that she had a date with Timmy, knowing that it would please her and keep her from asking too many questions. MawMaw beamed and left her to finish getting ready.

Sarah was outside, waiting for Timmy when he pulled up in his father's car. He had a beautiful bouquet of flowers for her, and she was impressed that he had a car for them. Timmy could tell that she was happy and said, "See? I did all of this for you!" "Yes, I see," Sarah said. "Now, let's go to the Mill." As Timmy looked into her blue eyes, he felt like she had never looked more beautiful than she did at that moment.

It took them about forty-five minutes to drive to the Mill. The travel time would have been less, but they had to avoid driving through certain neighborhoods. They pulled into the parking lot, and Sarah spotted the office sign and told Timmy to park close to it. She checked her makeup in her compact, then got out and told Timmy to wait there. He was confused but nodded and asked if he should keep them engine running. She shook her head and told him to turn it off—she might be a minute.

When Sarah entered the office, it was empty. She sat down and waited for about ten minutes then walked over to the front desk where she saw a bell with a note that said, "Please ring this bell, and have a seat. Someone will be with you shortly." Sarah rang the bell and sat back down. A middle-aged White man came from behind the door and asked how he could help her. "I'm looking for Mr. Andon. Is he here?" "Andon Augustin?" he asked. Sarah didn't know Andon's last name, but she assumed they were talking about the same person. "Yes, sir," she said.

The man asked her who she was, and she told him that she was Andon's girlfriend. He frowned and repeated what she said just to be sure he heard her correctly, then said that Andon wasn't there. Sarah said, "He does work here, doesn't he?" The man nodded. "Then where is he?" she asked, visibly annoyed. The man said, "He is not here, and that is all I can tell you. Have a good day." He turned and walked away, ignoring Sarah as she attempted to ask him another question.

Sarah walked out. She was concerned about Andon, and she was frustrated that the man wouldn't tell her where he was. As she walked toward the car, a young woman came out after her. She asked if Sarah was looking for Mr. Augustin, and she nodded. "He had to go back to

Haiti. There was a storm. His parents were killed, and his family lost everything. We don't know when he will be back. Sarah gasped, then thanked the young woman and introduced herself. "It's nice to meet you, Sarah. My name is Charlotte."

CHAPTER
FIFTEEN

TWO months had passed since Sarah visited the Mill. She had given up hope on ever seeing Andon again, assuming that he must have stayed in Haiti. She started dating Timmy. She didn't like him much in the beginning, but he slowly started to grow on her, just as her grandmother had hoped. Timmy would drive her to work most days; but one day, his father needed the car, so Sarah took the bus.

Sarah was stunned as she watched Andon get on the bus. She was so happy to see him, but he didn't notice her or how frantic with excitement she was. He was busy ensuring that the woman and the small child she had with her were seated before he paid their fare. Once he did so, he went to sit down next to them. They played with the baby and talked. They appeared to be comfortable with one another and the child. Sarah watched them, trying to figure out who the woman and child were. She hoped maybe it was his sister, but then Andon got up. Sarah knew this wasn't where he usually got off the bus, so she watched as he picked up the baby and helped the woman from the seat. He walked them to the front of the bus and as they got off, they kissed, and the lady said goodbye with a heavy accent and told the baby to wave to daddy.

Sarah was crushed. She felt as though her heart had stopped beating. All that she had hoped for was now gone. She was so sure that she and Andon would be together once he returned, and she had convinced herself that he wanted her as much as she wanted him. She felt betrayed, like he had lied to her. She felt like he had deliberately kept it from her that he had a woman and a baby. All the talking they had done, and he had never mentioned them.

Sarah got off at her stop. She would usually cross the street as soon as the bus let her off; but this time, she let the bus pass her. She wanted to look at Andon, hoping he would see her too. They locked eyes as the bus pulled off and stared until the bus was out of sight. Sarah was a wreck after discovering Andon already had a family. A family that she had dreamed would be hers.

Things between her and Timmy had cooled off since she had seen Andon with his family, and she barely wanted to see him at all. He got tired of her on-again-off-again attitude and decided he was done with her. For several weeks, Sarah went to work and came home, staying in her room and not engaging with MawMaw much. MawMaw noticed her behavior and asked her about it one night before they went to bed.

"What's the matter with you, child? You've been moping around like a hurt dog. What's going on with you? Are you and Timmy, okay?" "I'm not interested in seeing him anymore," Sarah said. "I see. You are heartbroken," MawMaw said. Sarah shook her head. "Well, what is it, honey? You know you can talk to me about anything. Is it someone else?" Sarah looked at her grandmother and said, "How did you know?" "Because you just told me," MawMaw laughed. "So, you're seeing someone else?" Not really, MawMaw. I want to but..." "When you want something, you have to go after it. Don't let anything stop you from getting whatever or whoever it is. You understand me?" MawMaw cupped Sarah face in her hands. "We've been stifled enough. The White man tells us what we can and can't do. We are told we're not good enough. We can't do certain things because we're women. Enough of that! We are Lavenders. When we want something, we get it...by any means necessary. And don't you ever forget that. Now pick yourself up, girl. I had better never see you moping around here again, giving up on yourself and what you want. Go get it!" That was all the encouragement Sarah needed to go after what she wanted.

Sarah knew now she couldn't just go to Andon and profess her love for him. She needed to come up with a plan first. She watched Andon and his family for months. They had the same routine every day. They would get on the bus, then she and the baby would get off the bus and Andon would go to work. Andon wouldn't talk to her much after his family got off, no matter how much she tried. He kept the conversation to a minimum. She felt like she wasn't getting anywhere with him, so she started to talk to his wife. Sarah would get off the back of the bus while Andon walked his family to the front. She would strike up a conversation with her, pretending to be friendly just to find out all she could about her.

She found out that she worked in a Creole restaurant. It was owned by another Haitian family who had come to New Orleans for a better life. She was allowed to take Andon Jr. with her as there were older women who would help take care of the children while the mothers in the restaurant worked. Sarah learned that she came back with Andon because their home in Haiti had been destroyed in a hurricane. She also told her that she lived in the house with Andon's family. Sarah knew that Andon's parents had died, but his sister and two brothers had also lost their lives in the hurricane. Their home was directly in the path of the storm, and nothing could have saved it. The Augustin family had known ahead of time that the storm was coming and that their house was in danger; however, their parents were proud and had survived many storms before, so they decided to stay and ride it out. They had believed that this storm, like the others, would pass. The parents had encouraged the rest of the family to leave and seek shelter elsewhere, so she took her son and went to her family's home in a nearby town, but their three children had stayed. None of them wanted to leave their parents, and they all died. When Andon heard the news, he left New Orleans and went back to Haiti so he could bury his family. It took weeks after the storm to find their bodies and their home was destroyed. It didn't even look like there had been a home there. All that was left was a pile of dirt, rubble, and debris.

Andon would not leave until he found all his family members. The search party tried convincing him to give up, but he wouldn't because he was determined to give his family a proper burial. They found his parents first. They were under what had been the back of the house, holding hands. Three days later, Andon found one of his brothers and his sister huddled together not far from their parents. Two weeks later, they finally found his other brother, who had died trying to save his family. Andon was able to bury all his family members before he returned to the US.

She told all of this to Sarah and talked about how losing all his family members had taken a toll on him. Once he reunited with her and their son, he felt that life was worth living again and begged her to come back to the United States with him.

Sarah let this go on for about two months before she went to MawMaw to ask for advice on how to physically remove someone without touching them. She knew her grandmother's history and hoped that she could show her what to do.

One night, while they were eating dinner, Sarah said, "MawMaw? How can I get someone out of the way who is interfering in my business? There is this girl who is stopping me and my boyfriend from moving forward with our relationship." "Well, you could simply tell her to get out of the way," MawMaw said. "I tried that. She just keeps popping up." "What does your boyfriend have to say about all of this?" MawMaw asked. "Well, he is being patient with her. They have a history, and he doesn't want to hurt her feelings."

"That doesn't make sense," MawMaw said. "If he was serious about your relationship, he would tell her to push on. Is he still seeing her?" "No. They are from Haiti. She came here with him. But he tells me he is done with her. She keeps coming around because she doesn't have family here." "Oh, I see," MawMaw said. "So, he feels responsible for her?" "Yea, I guess so. I really want her to go back to Haiti, but I know she won't. What can I do, MawMaw? She's really starting to get on my nerves." MawMaw stared at Sarah for a minute. "There is something you could do, but you won't be able to undo it. Do you understand?" Sarah nodded.

The following day, Sarah got off the bus when Andon's wife and son did just as she had been doing for the past couple of months. She waited until she entered the restaurant then walked in and sat down. The waitress came to take her order, and she asked for a glass of water, and then asked if she could see her friend. Sarah had never asked for her name. She didn't care to know it. "My friend just came in here with her baby. Can you ask her to come here?" The waitress went to the back and came out with Andon's wife who was looking confused until the waitress pointed to Sarah. She smiled and walked over to the table. "Hello, Sarah. How are you today?" "I'm doing well. I just wanted to stop by and check on you before I went to work." "Oh, you're so sweet. Thank you. I just got here not long ago. I'm getting ready to start my shift." "I like your hair," Sarah said. Andon's wife looked surprised. "Really? You like my hair?" She laughed and said, "It takes a lot to tame it—that's why I keep it braided like this. I like your hair too," she said to Sarah. "I wish mine was more like yours."

She sat down and examined Sarah's hair, and Sarah did the same. She rubbed her fingers along her braids and said, "How do you braid it like this?" "I could show you, but not right now because I have to get to work." "No, that's okay. I think if I could look at and touch it, I could see how you did it." Sarah took a small pair scissors from her purse and tucked them under her sleeve. She cut one of the braids and tucked it and the scissors back into her sleeve. "Oh. I see how you did it. I'm going to try to do my hair like this when I get home later." Andon's wife laughed. "I can't wait to see how it turns out." Sarah said goodbye and headed out the door.

When Sarah got home, she went into MawMaw's room and handed her a paper bag with the braid in it. MawMaw looked at her and said, "Are you sure you want to do this?" Sarah shook her head. "If I do this, it can't be taken back." "I know," Sarah said. "I want her gone." MawMaw motioned Sarah out of her bedroom and closed the door behind her. A few minutes later, Sarah smelled something burning. She went to her grandmother's door and heard her chanting in a language she had never heard her speak before. She went back to her bedroom and fell asleep.

The following day, Andon got on the bus with his family, seated them, and then went to pay their fare. They acted as they normally would; and when it was time for them to get off, Andon walked them to the front of the bus and kissed them, then sat back down to read his newspaper. Sarah waited for a few minutes, then moved to the seat next to him and started talking. As the days went by, she noticed that his wife's health began to decline. She looked sicker and weaker each day. Andon started getting off the bus with her and walking her across the street into the restaurant. The bus driver would wait for him and wouldn't charge him another fare when he got back on the bus. Sarah could tell that Andon was deeply troubled by his wife's illness. She pretended to be concerned while she consoled and encouraged him until her stop came.

One day, there was a different bus driver. Andon pleaded with the driver to wait for him, but he wouldn't. Sarah got up and offered to walk his wife and son to the restaurant. "Are you sure?" Andon asked. "Yes. I'll do this for you," Sarah said. Andon was relieved as he had to get to work and didn't want to be late. Andon's wife looked at Sarah and smiled and said, "Hey, where have you been?" but she could barely speak. Andon didn't realize his wife knew Sarah. He was just appreciative to Sarah for helping to get them off the bus. Sarah picked up the baby and took the wife's hand, then helped them across the street. When they entered the restaurant, two women were waiting at the door for them. One of them grabbed the baby and the other took Andon's wife's hand, and they took them to the back of the restaurant. Behind the kitchen was a room with four small children, one in a baby crib, and an older woman who appeared to be taking care of them. On the other side of the room was a cot. They helped Andon's wife lay down and then one of them rushed past Sarah and into the kitchen. She came back shortly with a bowl of soup and began to feed it to her. Sarah watched everything and no one seemed to notice that she was standing there.

"What are you doing here?" Sarah turned to see the waitress who had helped her the last time she was there. "I was just making sure my friend was okay." "Your friend?" the waitress said as she brushed past her. "Get out of here. This is not your business." Then she and the other women in the room began to talk to one another in French. Sarah left the restaurant and went to work.

The next day, Andon got on the bus alone and Sarah went to talk to him. He hugged her and thanked her for helping him. He talked about how the illness came out of nowhere and said that the women in the restaurant thought that his wife was homesick. He disagreed, because she had been there for so long and thought that it had to be something else.

He said that he couldn't take her to the doctor because they didn't have money to cover medical expenses. They wanted to keep her at the restaurant so they could help her get better, and they said that traveling back and forth would only make her worse. "Did they keep your son there too?" Sarah asked. "Yes. There are other children there, and I can't take care of him without my wife, so I felt it would be best if he stayed there too. I'm going to see them when I get off work." "You're such a good father and husband. They are very lucky to have you," Sarah said. "Yea, we're lucky to have each other. I don't know what I would do without my wife. I hope she gets better," he said. But Sarah knew that she wasn't going to get better.

Sarah continued telling Essie the story. "Eventually, she passed away, and Andon and I grew closer. Andon Jr. was two years old when I got pregnant with Sara, and shortly after that, we moved in together. I am the only mother he has ever known." "Oh my God, Ma! That's horrible. How could you do something like that?" Essie asked. "I was young." "So, your grandmother killed his wife?" Essie interrupted. "Yes, we killed her," Sarah said as she buried her face in her hands and cried. Essie watched her in disgust. "I just can't believe what you're telling me right now." She got up from the table and left her mother sitting there.

Essie sat on the couch and watched the sun come up. She was overwhelmed with what she had heard but she was more concerned about

Andontis because he hadn't come home. Knowing what he would eventually succumb to, she could not go back to sleep or get rid of the thoughts that were crowding her mind. She heard Livi cry and went to get her, but Naomi was already up and getting her out of her crib. "Good morning," Essie said. "Morning, Es," Naomi said as she grabbed Livi. "You're up early." "I couldn't sleep," Naomi said as she walked to the kitchen to get Livi a bottle. Sarah was still sitting at the table, staring off in a daze. She didn't even realize that Naomi and Livi were there. "Are you okay?" Naomi asked her. Sarah jumped and said, "Yes, I'm fine. I am just a little tired. I didn't get much sleep last night." "Essie said the same thing. I'm glad I don't have what y'all have, because Livi and I slept well," Naomi said jokingly.

"I'm going to look at two houses later, so I'll be a little late getting home today," Naomi said. Sarah had forgotten that they had agreed to move. "Oh okay. I forgot all about that." Naomi looked concerned. "You do still want to move, right?" she asked Sarah. "Yes, I do. We could use a change. What did the appraiser say about this house?" "He said that the house isn't worth much of anything without an upgrade." "I figured that. This house is so old," Naomi handed the baby to Sarah as she went to get ready for work.

Later that day, Sarah put Livi down for a nap, and she began to drift off as well. This was her normal routine—she would nap when Livi napped. Plus, she was exhausted from being up all night. As soon as she got to sleep, she was awakened by a knock at the door. She jumped up, her heart pounding so hard and loudly that she could hear it. She was expecting it to be bad news about Andontis. She opened the door, and the appraiser was standing there.

"Can I help you?" she asked. "Hello, ma'am. I'm looking for Ms. Lavender." "I am Ms. Lavender," she said. "Oh, I'm talking about the Ms. Lavender that's selling this house." Then Sarah frowned. She said crossly, "She isn't here," and started to close the door. The appraiser stopped her by pushing the door back open. She looked at him like he was out of his mind. "Ma'am, I'm sorry. I'm Mr. Matthews. I appraised your house." "And?" Sarah said. "And I want to make you an offer." "What?" Sarah said shortly. "I want to make you an offer," he repeated. "An offer for what?" Sarah asked, aware of what he was talking about. "For your house, ma'am." "We aren't selling," Sarah snapped. "Excuse me?" "You heard me! I said we aren't selling!" She slammed the door in his face. The noise woke Livi, and Sarah went to her room to tend to her. Andontis came through the backdoor.

CHAPTER
SIXTEEN

OVER the next few weeks, Naomi noticed a change in Sarah and Essie. They seemed stressed and not like themselves. She had the afternoon off one day and was at home when her mother came in from work. "Hey, Ma. How are you feeling?" she asked Sarah. "I'm fine, darling. How are you?" Sarah replied. "I'm good. It seems like something has been bothering you and Essie. If you have changed your mind about moving, we can stay here." "No, no. I want to move. I can't wait until we get out of this house," Sarah said. "Oh, okay. I believe that this move will be good for all of us." Naomi said, and Sarah nodded.

"I'm close to making a decision. I have narrowed it down to two places: a house and an apartment. Both have four bedrooms. The house has a full basement, two bedrooms on the first floor, and two upstairs. The apartment has a living room, dining room, a full kitchen, and one-and-a-half bathrooms. It is much cheaper than the house, and the heat is included. Both are in good neighborhoods, but the apartment is closer to Essie's store. I wanted us to go see them so that we could decide together." "Wow, Naomi. You are on it. I'm not surprised at all. You've always been my most resourceful child. Do we have to put any money down?" Sarah asked. "Yes, but I can take care of that. We will all have to chip in on the rent or the mortgage." "That's fine with me. I have money saved up, and I know Essie does too," Sarah replied.

Later that evening when Essie came in from work, the family was in the living room watching Livi take her first steps. Livi took a couple of steps toward Andontis, who was holding her pacifier to persuade her to walk to him. Essie and Sarah had forgotten about the grief they both felt regarding the fate of their family. Naomi, totally unaware of this, said "I'm happy we're all here. I found two places for us and would like to know if we could all go see them so we could make a decision as a family." "What places?" Andontis said. "We're moving. Didn't you know?" Naomi asked. "No, but I'm glad we are. I don't need to see them. Whatever you all decide, I'm cool with it. I'll be leaving for college anyway, but I'm still happy about moving out of this old house," he said.

The three women agreed to move into the apartment. It had plenty of space, and they all had their own rooms. The apartment needed some repairs, and the new landlord agreed to fix everything before they moved in. He guaranteed that the repairs would be done in a couple of weeks, and Naomi paid the deposit to secure it for them. They were all excited about the move. Sarah was excited, but she wanted to keep the old house for reasons only she knew. Naomi had forgotten all about selling the house after meeting with the appraiser, and Sarah didn't tell her that the appraiser had offered to buy it.

Essie continued her studies, but after her conversation with Sarah, her grades started to slip. She attended all her classes but couldn't focus on the assignments. She worried about her brother. Although she knew that there wasn't anything she could do to stop it, she became obsessed with keeping up with Andontis. She wanted to hang out with him all the time, and she wanted to know where he was and who he was with. This frustrated him so much so that he started to avoid her. He felt like she was prying and treating him like a child, and he didn't appreciate it. One night, they were closing the store, and he was planning to spend time with Franny. He knew that Essie would try to change his mind, so he finished what he needed to do and left without telling her. When she realized Andontis had left, she panicked.

Locking up the store in a hurry, she forgot that she was counting down the register to take the deposit to the bank and left the register and all the money that she'd counted out in the open. Anyone who passed the store would be able see the money from the outside. Essie got home as quickly as she could. She burst through the front door, startling Naomi. "Is Andontis here?" she asked Naomi. "He came by to get some clothes, but he left again," she said. "What's wrong?" "Nothing is wrong. He just left the store without telling me," Essie said and started ranting about how irresponsible he was.

Naomi looked at Essie, not understanding why she was so upset. "Well Essie, he is growing up, and he doesn't need to be monitored." "He does need to be monitored!" Essie yelled. She and Naomi began to argue, with Naomi telling her that she didn't need to act like his mother and Essie yelling at Naomi to stop talking about things that she didn't understand. While they were arguing, Sarah came in. "What is going on?" she asked. "Ask your daughter," Naomi snapped. "What's the matter, Essie?" Essie started yelling at Sarah. "You know what's going on, and it's all your fault!" Essie hurled hurtful words at her mother, and Naomi didn't understand what was happening. Then Sarah slapped Essie. "You won't talk to me like that. I am your mother!" she yelled. The slap caught Essie off guard and surprised Naomi. Neither of them had ever seen that side of Sarah. Essie placed her hand on her face where Sarah's hand landed, then she stormed out of the house. Naomi started to go after her, but Sarah grabbed her arm. "Let her go," she said. Sarah knew what was bothering Essie, but she knew she couldn't tell Naomi because she was too fragile to handle it. She felt like Essie was the strongest out of all four kids, not including Andon Jr., since he was not from her bloodline.

Andontis spent most of his time with Franny. Her mother allowed him to stay at their house whenever he wanted. He had become part of their family. He ate dinner with them, went on family outings with them, and had met a lot of their family members. They all admired Andontis. They liked how respectful he was and how well he treated Franny. They felt that he was a good match for Franny because he worked and was going to college. Franny's mom knew that he would be a great husband and father, so she pushed Franny to make him happy. And she did. Andontis was smitten. After all he'd gone through with Shelly, Franny treated him with love, kindness, and respect.

One evening after dinner, Andontis and Franny were in her backyard, resting on the hammock. "You've basically met my entire family. When will I get to meet yours?" she asked him. "You could meet them whenever you want to. We're getting ready to move to a new place not too far from here. Maybe we could plan something for our families to meet?" "That would be a great idea," Franny said. "Where are you all moving to?" "Cladney Street. It's a couple of blocks from here," he said.

"Hey, Mom. I think we should cook dinner for Andontis and his family," Franny said to her mother as they prepared dinner. "He said they are moving close by. We should invite them over once they settle into their new place. He's met everyone in our family, so we think it'll be a good way for us to get to know each other." "I agree," her mom said. "Where is he tonight?" "He's at home helping his mom and sisters pack."

Andontis was in the attic, packing up his things. He had been home all day to help since he hadn't been there much. He started to clean out a closet space in the attic that he'd never used. Most of the things that were in it belonged to his oldest sister, Sara. As he got to the bottom of the closet, he noticed a shirt that had belonged to her that was stained with what looked like blood. He hadn't seen Sara in years and finding this shirt troubled him. He went downstairs to talk to Sarah about it. "Mom, do you talk to Sara?" he asked. "Yes, I talked to her about a week ago," Sarah said. "Why do you ask?" "I found this bloody shirt of hers in the closet upstairs." Sarah took the shirt from Andontis and examined it. She knew exactly how the shirt got blood on it…and whose blood it was. It wasn't her daughter's blood though. "You never know what happened. She was always a mystery. I'll just throw it away," Sarah said. As Andontis headed back to the attic to finish cleaning and packing up, he wondered why Sara wasn't around.

As Andontis packed, he found more things that belonged to his oldest sister. The most disturbing item he found was the bloody shirt. The second was a notepad filled with drawings and notes. Finding the notepad was not as disturbing as what was in it. It was filled with hate and disdain for her family and creepy drawings. There were pages about killing the entire family by burning the house down while everyone slept. There were many things written about killing herself as well. The notepad was filled with hatred for Sarah, but there was a part about him too. She wrote about hating him and hating that she had to take care of him while her parents worked. She said her mother was a jealous witch. She called Naomi stupid, Essie a sneaky snake, and A.D. a sissy. Andontis noticed that there was no mention of their father who was now absent from his life as well. He stopped reading. He was upset with his sister and thankful that she wasn't around. He decided not to share what he had found. He put the notepad in a box of things that he planned to take to college with him. He was going to get rid of it, and he didn't want to take a chance on his sisters or Sarah finding it. He felt that it was just as hurtful as it was hateful, and he didn't want to put his family through that.

That evening, Naomi brought dinner in from a local restaurant in celebration of their upcoming move. Andontis, Sarah, and Naomi gathered around the table and Livi was in her highchair. Essie came in later and didn't bother joining them. She didn't even speak when she came in. Andontis and Naomi had noticed how different Essie had been acting for the past couple of weeks. Sarah noticed too but she knew why her daughter would be sad for a moment, angry for another, and a nervous wreck other times. Her behavior had become so inconsistent and erratic that Naomi thought she was losing her mind. Andontis didn't know what was up with her. He tried his best to avoid her because he felt like she was trying to control his life.

Essie's recent behavior reminded Sarah of her own when she lost control of things, and she felt bad for her. She should not have involved her in the messy history of the Lavender bloodline, but she needed her strongest child to know and understand what was coming and how to handle what was on their family.

The landlord finally completed all the repairs on the new apartment. Naomi went to pick up the keys and got copies for everyone. She was so excited and couldn't wait to let them all know that they could start to move their things to the new place. Since the new apartment was near Essie's store, Naomi decided to stop by to share the news with her. She hadn't seen much of her lately; and when she was around, she had been withdrawn and standoffish. Naomi hoped that the news would lighten her mood and give her something to smile about.

Naomi walked into the store but didn't see Essie. She walked to the register and said, "Hello. I'm Naomi, Essie's sister. Is she here?" "Yes, ma'am," the young lady said and called Essie on the intercom. She came out of the back and saw Naomi standing there, smiling. Essie was relieved that Naomi wasn't there with any bad news. "Hey, Es," Naomi said. "Hey. What are you doing here?" Naomi was giddy as she prepared to tell Essie she had the keys to the new place. "Is there somewhere we could talk?" she asked. "Yes. Follow me." Naomi followed Essie to the back office where she was sitting at her desk, doing homework before she was called to the front.

"What is it, Naomi?" "I got the keys!" Naomi said joyfully. Essie just looked at her. "Essie, aren't you happy about this?" Naomi asked. "We're finally moving out of that old house and into something better. A better neighborhood. A better environment!" "I am, Naomi. I just have so much on my mind, and it's becoming too much to bear." "Do you want to talk about it?" Naomi asked sympathetically. "I'm here for you, Essie. You know this, right?" She wrapped her arms around Essie and held her close. Essie sighed deeply and started to cry. Naomi didn't ask any more questions—she just held her baby sister. "Let it out, Essie. Let it out. It's going to be alright. You're going to be alright," Naomi crooned as she allowed her sister to rest in her arms—something she hadn't been able to do for a long time.

It took about three weeks to move everything into the new house. Everyone had moved in except Sarah. Every time Naomi asked when she would be moving in, she answered "soon." She had been to the new apartment many times, helping Naomi and Essie decorate. She even bought things for her bedroom and babysat Livi there. She had everything in her bedroom except her bed, and she used that as an excuse not to sleep there. She told Naomi that she had purchased a new bed and would move in once it was delivered. But she had not bought a new bed and had no intentions of moving to the apartment. She thought she was tainted and didn't want to leave too much evidence of herself there. Plus, she had plans that could only be carried out in the old house. What she needed to do had to be done in their house; the house where her mother and grandmother lived. The house where she and Andon had buried MawMaw. The land on which it was built belonged to them, the Lavenders. This detail had not been shared with Essie.

Essie spent a lot of time at the old house as well. She wanted to be alone, and she knew no one would be at the old house so she went there when everyone else was at the apartment. Many nights, Naomi was at the apartment alone with Livi. She found herself spending more time alone in the new house than she wanted to. She had never told her family how afraid she was to live alone. She didn't want to burden them, and she knew she had to get over her fear of being attacked again and left for dead. She had not seen or heard from Sebastian, and she did not want to. She knew he was the one who had tried to kill her, and she was afraid that he would someday return to finish the job.

One evening, while Essie was at the old house, she was laying on the couch in the living room and heard the back door open and close. She didn't bother to get up to see who it was. She was exhausted both mentally and physically. "You okay, baby?" She heard her mother's voice. "Yes, I'm fine," she said without looking up. Sarah took this as a sign that she wanted to be left alone so she went into her bedroom and shut the door behind her.

As Essie drifted off to sleep, she dreamed of a single tree in a huge field. Suddenly, lightning struck the tree from the night sky, and it began to burn from the top. A line of fire traveled down to the bark of the tree.

Essie felt her feet grow hot as the grass she was standing on started to burn. She thought it strange because she was nowhere near the burning tree. She watched as a single line of fire extended from the top to the bottom of the tree and then split into multiple lines that disappeared into the soil. The heat under her feet intensified, and she started to run. Then she woke up. She touched her feet as she sat up on the couch, and they were hot, as was the rest of her body. She was sweating, so she got up to get a glass of water from the kitchen. She peeked into her mother's room and saw that she was sound asleep, so she decided to stay there for the night. When Essie got up the next morning, she wanted to tell her mother about the dream she had had, hoping she could help make sense of it, but Sarah had already gone to the new apartment to babysit for Livi.

"When is your new bed being delivered so you could actually wake up here instead of having to travel here so early every morning?" Naomi asked her mother as she handed Livi to her. "They said sometime soon. I have to call them to check," Sarah said. "Has Andontis been here?" "Yes, he was here last night, but he was gone when I got up this morning." Sarah said, "He's been spending a lot of time with that girl." "Yes, he has. He wants us all to meet her family and have dinner soon. He told me last night that Franny and her mom were planning a big dinner for us. Did you know they were Puerto Rican?" "Honey, I had no idea," Sarah said.

Essie came in a little while later. She said hello to Naomi and then went to play with Livi. "Hey, Ma. I didn't know you left this morning. You should have woken me up. Has Andontis been here?" she said to Sarah. "I didn't know that you wanted to be woken up," Sarah said. "Naomi said he was here last night but gone this morning. Stop worrying about your brother, Essie. He will be fine." Essie looked at her and frowned, then shook her head. "See you later," Naomi said. She kissed Livi and left. After Naomi was gone, Essie handed Livi back to Sarah and went to her bedroom. Sarah followed her. "Essie, I know this is hard, but you have to…" "I don't want to talk about it," Essie snapped before she could finish.

As Andontis and Franny slept, Franny's mother knocked on the door and let herself in. "I cooked breakfast guys. Come eat while it's still hot," she called. "Coming, Mami," Franny said, still half asleep. They got to the kitchen table, and she had prepared a huge spread for them. Franny's three siblings were already at the table. This kind of thing was normal in their household. Their family loved to cook, and they always prepared more than any of them could eat.

"Franny, would you like to say grace?" her mother asked. "I want to say grace," said Miguel, Franny's younger brother. "God, thank you for the food Mommy prepared for us today. We thank you for the nourishment it will provide to our bodies. In Christ Jesus' Name. Amen." Franny ended the prayer and everyone else around the table echoed, "Amen." "And thank you Jesus for bringing my daddy back home. Amen." Miguel ended his prayer as well. This was something that Andontis loved about Franny and her family. They included him in everything that they did. He loved Franny and loved spending time with her and her family. He loved his family too, but this was different. He felt safe and at peace with them.

"Do you have to work today, Donti?" asked Franny's mom. "Yes, I do but not until later." "Are you excited about college? That's so amazing that you get to go. You know, a lot of us haven't had that same opportunity—you should take full advantage of it. We don't see things like this happen too often around here, you know." "Yes, ma'am. I am very excited," Andontis said. "When do you leave?" "Next month," he said. "We are going to throw you the biggest going away party!" Franny's mother exclaimed. "That will be great, ma'am," Andontis said. "It will be the perfect chance for our families to meet." "I was hoping we could meet them sooner than next month. And please Donti, stop it with the 'ma'am.' We're family—call me 'Mami.'" "Okay," Andontis said. "We are all moved in, so we can do it next week. I have to see what my sister's schedules are, and I'll let you know." "Franny and I are going to cook and plan the whole thing. Right, mija?" she said as she squeezed Franny's cheeks and kissed her. "Yes, Mami," Franny answered.

While Franny and her mom finished clearing the table and doing the dishes Miguel, Adrianna, and their younger sister went into the family room to watch cartoons. Andontis had left and gone home. "Mija, what's wrong? You seem like something is bothering you." "I'm okay. I am just worried about where our relationship will go after he's in college. He will be away, and there will be other girls at college. "Oh, mija. I don't think you have to worry about that. Donti loves you. You just have to be sure to do all you have to do to keep him happy. He won't need another girl if you do that."

Franny's mother was projecting her own beliefs onto her daughter. She blamed herself for her husband leaving even though he didn't treat her well. He was an alcoholic who cheated on her all the time. He would come and go as he pleased, and she never gave him any grief about it. The last time he left, he went back to Puerto Rico where he had another family. He had been gone for eight months, but Franny's mom was always hopeful that he would come home. The longest he had ever been gone was eighteen months. When he came back, they conceived the baby girl who was now three years old. She barely knew her father, but the other two children did, and they missed him so much. They too were hopeful for his return. Franny didn't care whether he came back or not. She just wanted her mom to be happy. Her mother wouldn't date or even look at another man. She was totally committed to her husband, even though he wasn't committed to her.

When Andontis got home, Sarah and Livi were in the living room, watching cartoons. "Hey, baby," Sarah said. "I heard we will be meeting Franny's family soon." "Oh yea, her mom thought it would be a good idea for us to get to know each other as a family," He said," "I agree. Since you spend all of your time with them, I think it is only fair that I meet the family who's stealing my baby boy away," Sarah teased. Andontis blushed as he played with Livi. "They aren't stealing me away, Ma." He went to his bedroom to relax. He looked around at the boxes he still had sitting there and decided to unpack and pack at the same time. He separated the things he wanted to leave there from the things he needed for college. Realizing that he had left the box with all of his sports gear at the old house, he called, "Hey, Ma? I left some stuff at the house. I'm going over there now. Do you need anything?" "Let me get Livi ready, and we'll go with you," Sarah said. "That's okay. I'm coming right back. You will just slow me down." They both laughed. "I need to get back here so I can relax before I go to work." "Okay, baby," Sarah said as she watched him leave, not knowing if she would see him alive again.

Andontis got to the old house and found the box he was looking for in the attic. As he was coming down the stairs, the telephone rang. He wondered why his mom hadn't gotten the telephone service transferred to their new apartment. "Hello? Hello, Andontis? Is that you?" Andontis frowned at the voice on the other end of the telephone. "Yes, it's me, Shelly. What do you want, and why are you still calling here?" "That's no way to talk to your girlfriend now, is it?" Shelly said in her perfect southern accent. "Shelly, we are not together. What are you talking about?" Andontis snapped. Shelly ignored him. "I was thinking that we should get together later. I miss you so much!" "Shelly, stop it okay? It's over between us. Stop calling here." "Why are you being so mean to me?" Shelly started to cry. "I only wanted to see you one last time. Is that too much to ask? Please can I see you? I *need* to see you, Andontis. I won't survive without you!" Andontis took a deep breath. "Okay, Shelly, but this is the last time."

Andontis arrived back at the apartment with his sports equipment. He stormed past Sarah and Livi, who were still sitting in the living room watching cartoons. He went to his room, dropped the box, and slammed his bedroom door. He was frustrated with himself for allowing Shelly to get to him, and he was upset that he had agreed to see her. He felt like it was wrong since he was with Franny now. He started to feel guilty and wanted to renege on the promise he made to meet Shelly, but he had no way to contact her, so he decided to stick with the plan and be done with her once and for all.

CHAPTER
SEVENTEEN

ESSIE scheduled herself and Andontis to work together that day because she hadn't seen him in a week. He was purposely avoiding her because he felt she was trying to control him, and he didn't like it. He felt like she had changed, and their once close relationship would dissolve if she kept it up. To his surprise, they got along just like old times during their shift. He felt like things were back to normal. He missed "this" Essie.

"So, are you ready to go to college and be miles away from us?" Essie teased. "Well, I am ready for college, but I am not ready to leave all my women!" he said, and they both laughed. "All your women?" Essie asked. "Yes! You, Mom, Naomi, Livi, and Franny!" "Oh, okay. You talking about 'all your women'...I thought maybe you had started pimping or something." They both chuckled. "I heard that we are supposed to be meeting Franny and her family," Essie said. "Yes. I wanted to talk to you and Naomi to figure out when would be a good time. I'm cool with whatever you all decide. We can talk to Naomi later and schedule the day," Andontis said. They were both relieved that they were talking— they had missed each other and the close bond that they had once shared. Essie was still on edge about what was to come, but she decided to embrace it and spend time loving on her brother because she knew there wasn't anything she could do to change his future.

Later that night, Naomi, Essie, Andontis, and Livi were at home, and Sarah had gone back to the old house to get some rest. Naomi bathed Livi and put her to bed. Once she was finished with her own bath, she pulled a small bottle of Canadian Reserve Whiskey out of her closet. She took two gulps and put it back in its hiding place. Andontis was laying on his bed, thinking about his meeting with Shelly. He badly wanted to cancel because he didn't want anything else to do with her. He felt guilty about agreeing to meet with her because he didn't want to do anything that would interfere with the good thing he had going on with Franny. Essie drifted off to sleep and started to dream about the burning tree again.

The flames were coming at her again. It was as if they were chasing her. She ran. While she was running, a flame passed her then circled back. Not knowing what to do and not having anywhere to go, she stopped running. Essie watched as the flame slowly crawled up her leg. It continued to trace her entire body like a spark, leading towards the fuse of a bomb. Essie watched and waited, knowing that it would soon engulf her. The flame suddenly stopped at her right hand. Turning her hand back and forth, Essie examined it. As she opened her hand, the flame disappeared, leaving behind a petal from a lavender flower. A rushing wind blew the petal toward the tree which was now forming a face in the smoke. Essie couldn't tell whose face it was. She started to feel heat in her belly. She looked down to see that she was on fire from her waist down to her feet. She screamed and woke up.

The next few days were peaceful in their home. Everyone was getting along so well, and they enjoyed spending time together. Especially Sarah, as she knew it was just a matter of time before the devastation hit. Andontis started spending more time at home, sleeping in his own bed. Essie had come to terms with what was going to happen. Although she experienced so much anxiety at the thought of losing her baby brother, she knew it was going to happen no matter what.

Andontis had made up his mind about his meeting with Shelly. He felt like he didn't owe her any explanation, and he was tired of the guilt and shame that overwhelmed him about agreeing to the meeting in the first place. The time had come and passed. Initially, he worried that Shelly would try to contact him; but after a couple of days with no word from her, he felt confident that he could move on.

One afternoon, Andontis and Essie were at the store. The next day, they were supposed to have dinner with Franny and her family. While Essie was in the back office studying, Andontis was in the store, stocking the shelves. Everything was peaceful—until Shelly walked into the store. She walked past the cash register, straight to where Andontis was working. "You lied to me!" she yelled. Andontis looked up and was shocked to see her standing there. He forced her to leave the store, pushing her out as she screamed and cried. Essie heard the commotion and went to see what was going on. Everyone in the store was watching as Andontis and Shelly argued. Shelly was kicking and punching him. Just as Essie made it outside to pull her off him, Andontis slapped Shelly across the face, and she fell to the ground. "I'm sorry. I didn't mean to do that," he said. Essie went to help Shelly off the ground, and Shelly lashed out at her. "Get off of me, nigger!" She ran off with a bloody nose and a scraped knee and elbow.

That evening, Essie and Andontis were getting ready to close the store. The young lady who worked at the cash register finished her shift and said goodnight. Outside, she noticed Shelly across the street. She didn't think much of it and went on without letting Essie or Andontis know. About an hour later, Andontis left the store and headed to Franny's to spend the evening with her. Essie stayed to finish closing. After she was finished, she locked the store and took the bank deposit. She decided to stay the night at the old house since it was closer to the bank. She could save a trip by taking it home with her and going to the bank when it opened tomorrow. As she walked, she spotted Shelly running away from the field that was a couple blocks away from their house. She thought it was strange that she was in the neighborhood this late.

Sarah could not fully register what Essie was saying. "Who killed who, Essie?" she kept asking. "It happened, Ma! It happened!" Essie sobbed. "He's gone! They killed him! Andontis is gone!" Sarah let out a cry that could be heard for miles. Falling to the floor, she and Essie sobbed hysterically as they held onto each other. "Where is he?" "He was in the field down the street." "I have to see him!" Sarah cried. They headed to the place where Essie last saw Andontis. When they got there, there was a crowd gathered. One of their neighbors met them before they got to the spot. "I'm sorry, Sarah. It's…Andontis. They killed him." Andontis was hanging from a tree with a bloodied face and gunshot wounds in his head and chest. "Get him down from there!" Sarah screamed. Essie couldn't believe what she was seeing. Her baby brother strung up; beaten, shot, and unrecognizable. A couple of their neighbors tried to console her. "Call the police," someone said. One of the men cut Andontis down from the tree, and Sarah held him in her arms and cried until she had nothing left.

The next morning, Naomi was getting ready for work and waiting for Sarah to come to take care of Livi. She was late, and Naomi was concerned because Sarah was never late. After an hour, Naomi called the mother of the child that she tutored every morning to let her know that she couldn't make it. Naomi didn't know what had happened, but she didn't mind staying home with her daughter. Later that morning, she put Livi down for a nap then went into the bedroom. She got the bottle of whiskey she'd been hiding and took a couple of sips. She heard someone come in the door. It startled her, and some of the whiskey spilled out on the floor and onto her clothes. She was trying to clean it up when Essie came in.

Naomi realized that something was terribly wrong. Essie reached out, grabbed her, and cried. Naomi asked her what was wrong, and she sobbed, "He's dead, Naomi! Andontis is dead!" "What? What do you mean, Essie?" Essie couldn't say another word; she just cried in Naomi's arms. Naomi still didn't understand what Essie was saying. She walked her sister out of her room so she wouldn't wake Livi and into the kitchen. Then she saw Sarah sitting there with blood all over her clothes. Naomi thought Sarah was bleeding and went over to her. She examined her mother, trying to find the source of the blood. "Ma, what happened? Are you alright?" Sarah didn't answer her. "Ma!" Naomi yelled. "What's going on?" Sarah looked at her and started to cry. "No, no, no." Naomi said as she backed away from Sarah. She covered her mouth and shook her head in disbelief. "No!" she yelled again as she backed into the fridge. She slid to the floor. All three of the Lavender women were sobbing. Essie was standing on the wall, Sarah was sitting in a chair at the kitchen table, and Naomi was on the floor in front of the refrigerator.

Franny and her mother were at home, making dinner for that night. Her mom went through the house, making sure everything was perfect and dressed the younger children in their best clothes. Franny was setting the table. She was concerned that Andontis hadn't come to see her the night before like he had promised. Hours passed without a word from him. Franny and her family sat around the table, waiting and waiting, and there was still no word from him. Later that night, as they cleared the table Franny cried, thinking that he had decided to leave her like she thought he would. Her mother tried to reassure her. "Don't worry, mija. He'll come back. They always come back."

Franny didn't get any sleep that night. She couldn't understand why he would do this to her. She decided to go to the store that morning. She got up, got dressed, and headed out the door. "Where are you going?" Her mother asked. "I am going to see Andontis at the store." Her mother smiled. She was glad that her daughter wasn't giving up on what she felt was a promising future. Franny entered the store and asked if she could speak to Andontis. The girl at the cash register looked at her strangely. Before she could tell her that he was dead, Mr. Melvin came out of the back. "Can I help you?" he asked Franny. "Yes, sir. I need to speak with Andontis." Mr. Melvin studied Franny and realized that she didn't know what had happened. "Follow me," he said sadly. When they got to the back office, Mr. Melvin asked her to sit down. "Are you his friend?" he asked her. "I'm his girlfriend," Franny said quietly. Mr. Melvin cleared his throat. "I am so sorry to be the one to tell you, but Andontis was killed two nights ago."

Franny sat still, dazed. "Can I drive you home?" Mr. Melvin asked. She nodded, still too stunned to speak. Mr. Melvin led her to his car. Franny got in and sat, staring at the dashboard. "Where do you live?" Mr. Melvin asked. Franny didn't say anything. He wasn't sure she could hear him, so he sat and prayed for her quietly. They sat in the car for forty-five minutes before Franny was able to tell him her address.

Mr. Melvin pulled up in front of Franny's home. He walked her to the front door and knocked. Franny was hysterical at this point. Her mother answered the door and said, "What's going on? Who are you? What's wrong with her?" She pulled Franny into the house and left the door open. Mr. Melvin followed her. "¿Quien es el señor, Francesca? ¿Te ha hecho algo?" "¡Andontis murió, Mami!" Franny cried. "¡El hombre dijo que alguien lo mató!" Mr. Melvin stood quietly. He assumed that Franny was telling her mother what happened, because he heard her say Andontis' name. Franny's mom was more disappointed than she was saddened. Not only were her daughter's hopes and dreams shattered... hers were too. The plans she had for her daughter were all for nothing. She ached for her daughter and for herself. "We are cursed," she said in Spanish.

Franny's mother got her calmed down, then took her to her bedroom to lie down. She offered Mr. Melvin a seat and asked if she could get him something to drink. He declined, then explained what happened. He also explained how he knew him. After they were done, Franny's mom walked him to his car. They shook hands, and she paid special attention to his left hand, noticing his wedding ring on his finger. She frowned and went into her home, slamming the door behind her. Mr. Melvin got in his car and drove back to the store.

After Andontis' death, Sarah lost herself. She didn't bathe. She stayed in the old house in her bedroom with the curtains drawn. She didn't eat or drink. She barely got up to use the bathroom. Essie and Naomi tried to comfort and console her and attempted to get her to come to their new apartment to be with the family—to no avail. It was overwhelming for both of them. After all, they were grieving too, but they still had to get up and continue. This is what their mother taught them. Essie reminded Sarah of this one night after trying to convince her to come home with her. Sarah just laid there in her bed in the dark, ignoring her pleas. Essie knew she couldn't help her mom, but she wanted to, so she kept at it, hoping that Sarah would come around at least before the funeral but she never did.

CHAPTER

EIGHTEEN

ANDONTIS' repast was held at the old house. The neighbors gathered to help them however they could. Andon Jr. was there with his wife and two children. Andon Sr. was there as well, but he stood off by himself and didn't talk to anyone. Andon Jr. and Naomi talked while he held Livi. Essie sat talking to Jeanie, who had heard about what happened and came to be there for Essie even though they hadn't seen one another for a while. "Thank you for coming, Jeanie. It means a lot," Essie said. "No mention. I love you, Essie, and I knew I needed to be here for you. I know I haven't always been a good friend to you, so this is the least I could do."

Sarah was in the bedroom alone. She was dressed entirely in black. She even wore a black veil which covered her face. Sarah didn't bother to greet the people who had come to support them—she went straight to her bedroom and stayed there. Naomi had gone into her mother's room several times to try and get her to come out, but Sarah refused to budge. She sat on the edge of her bed, staring at nothing. Mrs. Addie Frank joined her after a while. She sat next to her and put her arm around her shoulder. Sarah looked to see who it was, then broke down and cried. "My baby is gone, Addie. My baby is gone." Andon Sr. was on his way into the bedroom he used to share with Sarah just to talk to her and to feel her embrace once more. He saw Addie and decided not to interrupt. He left the house without saying anything to anyone and was never seen or heard from again.

"Jenn moved to Chicago last year and is doing really well. I am going in a few months," Jeanie said. "She is helping me get an apartment there. She lives in a place called "Standow Homes." She filled out an application for me and called last week to tell me that I was approved, so I'll be leaving soon. You can come too if you want. Even if you just want to get away from all this for a little while." "I would love to, Jeanie. I need a break. But I can't leave my mom and my sister. I don't think they could manage without me." "Just think about it. I will get you a bus ticket; and if you change your mind, you come whenever you want." Then Jeanie pulled out a joint and waved it back and forth in Essie's face. "For old time's sake?" she said. Essie smiled. "Let's go to the Barn."

Essie and Jeanie sat in Essie's old hiding spot at the back of the Barn reminiscing. Jeanie brought up James. "Have you seen him since that night?" "Yes, I ran into him a few times after that. He would go the other way whenever he saw me." They laughed. "Good." Jeanie said. "You saved my life that night, Essie. I could never thank you enough."

Later that evening, after the neighbors had left, Essie, Jeanie, and Naomi cleaned the house. Andon Jr., his wife, and children sat in the living room, playing with Livi. Sarah had not left her bedroom all day. She sat motionless in the same spot for hours. Andon Jr. went to check on her. He tapped on her door, but Sarah didn't move. She didn't even acknowledge that she had heard it. "Mom?" She still didn't say anything. He sat down next to her, and she looked at him with the saddest eyes he had ever seen. He knew there wasn't anything that he could say to take away her pain, so they sat in silence. Essie was putting something away in the kitchen when she noticed Sarah and Andon Jr. in the bedroom and went in to join them. She sat at Sarah's feet, placing her head in her lap. Naomi followed shortly after and sat on the other side of Sarah. They sat quietly, not talking. They knew this was what she needed. Maybe it was what they all needed and the only way to communicate it was to sit and say nothing, while the tears rolled down their cheeks.

"Daddy?" Andon Jr.'s baby girl stood in the doorway. She was three years old and the spitting image of Andon Jr. except for her eyes, which she had gotten from her mother. "Come here, baby." He reached for her, and she climbed into his lap. Sarah looked at her for the first time. "This is your grandma," Andon Jr. said to his daughter. "Mom, this is Sarah. Your granddaughter." Sarah smiled and said softly, "Hello, Sarah." This was the first time that she had shown any emotion since Andontis died.

Andon Jr. and his family stayed in New Orleans for a couple of days after the funeral. He wanted to spend some time with his family. They alternated between the old house and the new apartment. Sarah, still not herself, barely interacted with her children. She hadn't taken off the clothes she had worn to the funeral, and it had been two days. Andon Jr. was worried about her—he had never seen her like this. He knew she was hurting, but this was beyond anything he could have imagined. The night before he was scheduled to leave, he and his sisters decided to take the children to see Sarah. He remembered how there was a shift in Sarah's attitude when he introduced his daughter. They all agreed that it was a good idea, and Sarah was glad to see them. She doted on her grandchildren, and she seemed to be happiest when she was with the three of them. She didn't realize that Sara hadn't been there until Andon Jr. had asked about her. Then she remembered that she hadn't even told her that Andontis had died. "Oh, my goodness. I've been so overwhelmed that I forgot to call to tell her." Andon Jr. offered to call but Sarah declined, explaining that she was the only one who could deal with her these days. "I would love to speak to her though. Could I have her number? Where does she live?" Sarah was clearly uncomfortable with Andon Jr.'s questions. "Andon, it's best that you let me deal with this, okay?" "Is she okay?" he pressed. "She's fine, but she doesn't want us to contact her. She was clear with me about that." Andon Jr. was unsettled but decided not to push it any further. He and his family left the following day. They lived on the Army base in Fort Worth, Texas. They made plans for Sarah to come visit them in a couple of months, and Sarah agreed, even though she had no intention of going. She had other plans; plans that would shake the Lavender family down to its very core. She had convinced herself that it was what she had to do for the sake of her family.

A couple of months had passed since the funeral. Although Essie felt the void of losing her baby brother, she felt more at ease than she had since her mom told her about the curse. She no longer had to worry about Andontis and was able to move on with her life. She returned to work and school. Some days were better than others for her. Sometimes, she could get through an entire day without feeling the sting of her brother's death; while other times, she would withdraw from the world like Sarah did. She wouldn't leave her room, and wouldn't eat, drink, or bathe. She would stay in her room with the drapes drawn and wouldn't get out of bed. Naomi got used to the behavior and wouldn't bother her. She wanted to allow her sister to feel whatever she needed to feel in the moment.

Naomi moved on as well. She got a job as a teacher's assistant, even though she was responsible for teaching the class. The school where she worked was predominately White and would only allow her to work as an assistant. They didn't want Black women in leadership positions. A parent of one of the children that she tutored was the school administrator and referred her for the job. Naomi didn't mind it. She loved teaching, and she was making more money than she ever had, even though she wasn't being paid what she deserved. She continued to tutor part time. Some of her students did not need academic help anymore, but they would reach out to her occasionally for help with specific subjects or if they had a test coming up. She was paid well and was making a good living for her and her daughter.

Sarah never babysat Livi again after Andontis' death. She no longer possessed the mental capacity to take care of herself, and Naomi wasn't going to put her daughter in that kind of danger. Mrs. Addie Frank stepped in to keep Olivia while Naomi worked. She even allowed her to stay overnight on days she had worked late or was exhausted from dealing with the racism and oppression at the school. Sarah stayed at the old house, and Naomi and Essie would stop by often to check on her. She didn't go back to the new apartment—she was riddled with grief and guilt. She was so depressed that Naomi and Essie talked about taking her to see a doctor.

"Ain't nothing wrong with me," Sarah shouted at them when they tried to convince her to get help. "We're not saying that Ma," Naomi said. "There *is* something wrong with you!" Essie yelled back. "Look at you! Look at this room. There's no food in the house. You are as thin as a pole. This room is a mess. It stinks, and so do you. You haven't washed up in God knows how long. You obviously need to see someone!" When Essie went on her tangent, Sarah looked at her with her arms folded. She didn't seem upset or shocked—in fact she almost looked proud as she smirked at Essie. "I'm not going anywhere. I am staying here until I am good and ready. And I will be ready soon," Sarah said. When Naomi asked her what she meant, Sarah chuckled. Essie frowned and looked at her mother in disgust.

CHAPTER
NINETEEN

ESSIE recognized this field. There was something eerily familiar about it. There was a beautiful trail of lavender flowers, and she smelled smoke and heard the crackling sound of wood burning. It was dark. She followed the trail of flowers, and there was a tree burning. The top of the tree was totally engulfed in flames, but the trunk was not. Essie was closer to the tree than she had ever been, but she didn't move. She just stood there, watching the tree as it burned. She was so close that she could have reached out and touched it if she wanted to. Essie woke up in her bedroom. She looked over at the clock then lay there for a few minutes pondering on the familiar dream and wondering why she was dreaming about this again. She then got up to get dressed for work.

"Mr. Melvin, do you think God would try to tell us something through dreams?" Essie asked while the two were in the back office. "It's possible," he said. "Why do you ask?" "Well, I've started having this dream about a burning tree. It bothers me because I had this same dream a couple times before my brother was killed." Mr. Melvin leaned back in his seat and took a deep breath. "God does talk to us through dreams. But the dream could also just be that...a dream. If you want to be sure if He is talking to you, ask Him." "Ask Him?" Essie said. "Yes. Pray, and ask Him what, if anything, He is trying to convey." "I haven't prayed in a long time. Especially with all that has happened in my family," Essie said. "I understand," said Mr. Melvin. "But it doesn't hurt to ask Him."

He smiled, and Essie smiled back and continued making the schedule for her staff.

After work, Essie went to check on Sarah. When she got to the house, it was unusually cold and dark. "Mama!" Essie called. She called again, and Sarah didn't answer. She checked Sarah's bedroom, but she wasn't there...and then she noticed that the back door was open. She went to see if Sarah was outside and found her sitting on the backsteps. To Essie's surprise, Sarah had washed her hair and bathed. "Hey," Essie said as she sat down next to her. "Hey, Ester," Sarah said. She hasn't called Essie by her name in years. "Ester?" Essie replied. "That's your name, ain't it?" Sarah said, and they both smiled. "How are you feeling?" Essie asked. Sarah said that she was feeling better, and Essie said, "I learned in school that when someone's facial expressions or body language doesn't match what they're saying, it is usually not true." "I washed my hair and took a bath, so wouldn't you say I am better?" Sarah asked sarcastically, and Essie agreed that she had a point. "I have to talk to you," Sarah said. "Can I ask you something?" Essie asked at the same time. "You first," Essie said. "Go ahead," Sarah said, again at the same time. "I want to hear what you have to say Ma, so you go." Sarah took a deep breath. "What I have to say is going to take a while. So go ahead and ask your question."

Essie told Sarah about the dreams she had about the burning tree. She told her how often she had them and told her that the dreams started happening right before Andontis was killed. "What do you think it means?" she asked Sarah. "You know you are my strongest child," her mother replied. Essie stared, confused. "What does that have to do with the dream?" she asked. "I'm about to tell you," Sarah said. "When I was a child, my MawMaw told me a story about a Bible character called Esther. MawMaw wasn't spiritual by any means, but she did believe in God. I remember a short period of time when she was reading the Bible a lot and praying. There was this woman that used to come to our house after my mom passed, and she was a Jesus freak. I don't know how she met MawMaw, but she would come by a lot. I remember she would pray for her and was also teaching MawMaw about Him.

MawMaw would wake up praying. She would read her Bible, and she would also write stuff down in this folder she had. She would even pray for me. This went on for about five or six months. The lady used to try to convince MawMaw to come to church, but she would always refuse. When I noticed that she was not praying or reading her Bible anymore, I asked her about it.

"Baby, that type of thing just ain't for us. I know there is a God, but the stuff me and my family has done, the things we practiced on a daily basis…well, those don't go well with who He is."

That's when she told me about Esther. She told me that this lady was strong and that she led not only her family but her entire race to a place of peace, safety, and prosperity. She told me that all the other stories she read in the Bible mentioned God but not the story of Esther. MawMaw said she admired her. She talked about how beautiful and bold she was and about how she was married to a king and got him to change his mind about killing her people. She was smart and was ready to die for those she loved. She told me that I would have an Esther one day and that I would know it when she was born. And you, my dear Ester, were a stubborn baby. I carried you for exactly ten months. I was way over-due; and on the day I made it to ten months, you were ready! MawMaw told me that Esther prepared herself for ten whole months before she met the king.

When you came out, your right hand was balled up in a fist. The doctors thought that there was something wrong; maybe you had some type of deformity. When the doctors spanked you to make sure you were living and breathing, you wouldn't cry. But those blue eyes of yours were open and as bright as the day sky. When the nurse cleaned you up and handed you to me, you just glared at me. Not crying, not blinking…just staring. When I started to feed you, the right hand that you had closed so tightly began to open, and I felt like you reached out to me with it. You grabbed hold of my finger and would not let go. You nursed for a couple of minutes and fell asleep, still holding my finger. When the nurse came in to take you into the nursery, she tried peeling your hand from my finger, but you made it difficult for her. When she finally succeeded, that's when we all heard you cry for the first time. That's why I named you Ester."

"Wow, that's deep," Essie said. "Naomi was also named after a strong woman in the Bible, and there is a Sarah too. Even though your sister is named after me and MawMaw, I was happy that she would have a Bible name." "You never really talked to us about God or took us to church. Why did it matter so much to you to name us after people from the Bible?" Essie asked. "Because of the story of Esther. MawMaw said God wasn't mentioned in that story, but she believed that He was still there." "What does that have to do with my dreams about the burning tree?" Essie asked. "I wanted you to know where your name came from." "But why now? Why are you choosing to tell me this now?" Essie persisted. "Because I'll be leaving soon." Essie looked at her mother and frowned but didn't say anything. "Now let me tell you what all this has to do with your dreams," Sarah said.

"Remember everything I told you about my past, and the history of our family? That curse that was opened on our bloodline happened way before I was even born. There was no way to stop it or get around it. It was going to happen. That's just how it works. You can't undo it. After Andontis was born, I started reading my Bible and learning how to pray on my own. I was so in love with him, I couldn't stand knowing that he would someday be taken away from me. So, I began to study the Bible and study Jesus. What I'd come to know was that He is the most powerful thing on Earth and above it. If there wasn't a way to break the curse then surely, He could. I was convinced that He would save my baby from death. Then I kind of got the feeling that He wouldn't because I couldn't feel Him. He wasn't showing me that He heard me, and I got frustrated and gave up. When Olivia was born, I knew then that He had in fact heard me and that He had answered me. Naomi is free to have as many boys as she wants because her firstborn child was a girl.

When Andontis died, I was reminded that the curse still stands; and that even though God heard me, He wasn't going to interfere with what was already on our bloodline. The first male born to anyone with Lavender blood will die. That's the fate for this family, and the most unfortunate part. As I mentioned, this curse was birthed way before I was even born. There were many that came before me. My mother, MawMaw and her mother, and many other Lavender women practiced it…and they all misused it. Just as I misused it. I am the last one left of all of them who practiced…the last of the second generation. I am the only one left. So that tree you see in your dreams, Essie, is *me*.

That's why I have to go. There is no way to be sure that the curse won't follow you. You said that in your dreams the fire is chasing you, right?" Essie nodded. "It even caught you once, right?" Essie nodded again. "Where were those flames coming from?" Sarah asked. "The tree," Essie said, staring at Sarah and not moving. "If that tree isn't destroyed then the fire will get you," Sarah said. "Oh my God. Why is this happening to us? Why couldn't we just be a normal family? Did you know you would have to do this before I start having these dreams?" Essie asked Sarah. "Yes," Sarah replied. Essie broke down. "I can't take another loss. I can't. It's too hard." Sarah took Essie's face in her hands, wiping her tears with her thumb. "You are my Ester Renae Lavender. You're strong, bold, smart, and courageous. You will move on. You can finally live the normal life you want. You have your entire life ahead of you. You will get past this. Trust me. When you have your own daughters then you will understand why my going is necessary." "But what if I have a son?" Essie cried. "You won't. That's why we have to destroy the tree."

Essie was visibly shaken by what Sarah had just told her. Sarah had gone into the house and left her sitting on the stoop, and she sat and cried for hours. Sarah allowed her to get it all out without disturbing her because she knew that she needed this release before she could accept it. Essie finished crying, wiped her tears, and heard her mother's words play over and over in her head *"You're strong, bold, smart, and courageous. You can finally live the normal life you want. You will get past this. Trust me."* Essie got up and went to the bedroom where Sarah was lying down. Essie climbed into bed and laid in front of Sarah and snuggled. Sarah wrapped her arms around her and held her like she was a newborn baby. They both stared off into the air, both staring with the same posture and the same blue eyes, their hair pulled back into the same ponytail, almost identical except Essie was just a shade darker than her mother. They were at peace for the first time in a very long time.

The next couple of months were peaceful for the Lavenders, and everything appeared to return to normal. Essie returned to work and completed her degree. She decided not to participate in the graduation ceremony and waited for her degree and transcripts to come in the mail. Naomi was still working at the school and tutoring on the weekends. Olivia was walking and talking and knew how to say each of their names. She knew how to say her alphabet, could count to ten, and was learning to spell her name. Naomi was also teaching her colors. She was very advanced for a two-year-old. Sarah had started spending time at the new apartment again but still didn't stay the night. They made it a priority to eat dinner together.

One evening, Essie and one of the young ladies that worked in the store with her were talking as they closed the store. "I'm glad you're back, Essie. We missed you around here," the young lady said. "Aww, thanks. I am glad to be back." "Are the police still investigating Andontis' murder?" the girl asked. "I doubt it. We haven't heard anything from them in a while. They never take the murders of Black men seriously around here," Essie replied. "I know. It's a shame that they don't consider us real people. But I remember that night like it was yesterday. That White girl that your brother was dating was standing across the street when I left work. I thought it was strange that she was just standing there." Suddenly, Essie remembered that she had also seen Shelly that night, running from the field where Andontis was murdered. She grew quiet as she realized that Shelly was connected to Andontis' murder. "I'm sorry for bringing that up, Essie," the girl said as she noticed that Essie's demeanor had changed. Essie assured her that it was fine.

On the way home, Essie stopped at the spot where Andontis was killed. She stood there and cried. "I know there wasn't anything we could have done to stop this. But as sure as I live, I promise you, she's going to pay for this. I promise you, baby boy. I'm going to take care of her. I promise you. Her family will feel the same pain that we did." Essie said through the tears that were streaming down her cheeks. She headed home and arrived just as Sarah was setting out her plate for dinner. Sarah greeted her and noticed that she had been crying. She assumed that she knew why she was crying and decided not to ask her about it. Naomi came into the kitchen trailed by Livi, who climbed into the chair where Naomi usually sat. "Now you know you're not sitting there, little girl. Come here." Naomi picked Livi up to put her in her highchair. "No," Livi squirmed and tried to get down. Sarah laughed at her granddaughter. "She hates that thing now." Sarah said. "I'm a big girl," she said to Livi in the baby voice she used whenever she talked to her. They all sat down for dinner.

After dinner, Essie and Sarah cleaned up to kitchen, then Sarah left, and Essie went to bed. She couldn't sleep because she was overwhelmed at the thought of Shelly being the cause of Andontis' death. She became obsessed with finding Shelly because she knew that she had a connection to the guys that killed Andontis. After Essie drifted off to sleep, she dreamed of the tree again. It was fully engulfed in flames, and they once again began to chase her…but this time, she didn't run. She stood there watching as the flames got closer; but before they reached her feet, they suddenly went out. Essie's attention was then drawn to the tree that was starting to go out. Then she heard a pounding sound. She looked around but couldn't tell where the noise was coming from; then looked back at the tree, and it had burned all the way down to the stump and smoke was coming from it. Essie walked toward the place where the tree once stood and was now just a stump, covered in lavender flowers. She heard more pounding.

Essie was jerked awake as Naomi burst into her bedroom. "Essie, get up! Mama's house is on fire!" "What?" Essie said, shaking the sleep from her eyes. "They said Mama's house is on fire!" Essie threw her clothes on and followed Naomi out the door with Livi. As they grew close, they saw that the entire house was on fire. They heard the fire truck, and there were people standing all around. Naomi cried, "Where's my mother? Is she in the house?" Everyone looked around, confused. "My mother is in that house! Somebody help!" she screamed. She shoved Livi at one of the neighbors and tried to go into the house. Two of the men that were standing there grabbed her and stopped her. "Let me go! Please somebody help! My mother is in that house!" Naomi cried again. She screamed and fought the men who were holding her. When she realized that she couldn't get away from them, she fell to the ground, crying hysterically. Essie just stood there in shock, watching the house as it burned. She said to herself, "Why now? Couldn't you have given us more time?" as tears poured down her face.

The fire department forced everyone to move back as they set up their equipment, and one of them asked who lived in the house. "This is their house," a woman said and pointed to Essie. "What happened here?" the fireman asked her. "I don't know. I don't live here anymore, but my mother still does." "Where is your mother?" he asked. Essie looked at him sadly and didn't answer. "Is she still in the house?" he asked, and Essie nodded her head. The fireman ran back to the truck. "There's someone in the house!" Two of the firemen went inside to look for Sarah.

Minutes later, the firemen exited the house and Naomi ran over to them. "What are y'all doing? Where is my mother?" she cried. "I'm sorry, ma'am. We couldn't get to her." Naomi both of her hands over her mouth collapsed to the ground. "Oh my God! Mama, No!" Mrs. Addie Frank came and took her away from the crowd. When Naomi calmed down, she asked, "Where's my baby?" Essie walked up holding Livi, who was wide awake. Livi reached for her mother, and Essie held onto her as she reached out and grabbed her mother's neck. Essie put her other arm around Naomi, and Naomi broke down. Mrs. Addie Frank took Livi, and Essie held her sister as tightly as she could while she cried. Mrs. Addie Frank tried to convince them to come to her house. "I'm not going anywhere until they bring my mama out of there," Naomi said. "I'm going to stay here too," said Essie. "Can you please take Livi for us, Mrs. Frank?" Essie said, and Mrs. Addie Frank walked away with the baby.

It took the firemen into the wee hours of the morning to put the fire out. The sun was coming up and the fire was out, but the house was still smoking. A couple of the firemen had gone back in to try and find Sarah. Essie and Naomi sat at the back of one of the trucks and waited for them to come out. After about forty-five minutes, one of the men came out and walked over to the girls. "We found your mother." Naomi looked up. "I'm sorry. She is deceased. But there was someone else with her. Do you know who it could have been?" Naomi was too overwhelmed to hear what he was saying and didn't respond. "What do you mean?" Essie asked. "Someone else was there with your mother. We found your mother's body, and we also found the bones of another body in the house." Essie looked shocked, confused, and very puzzled as she mumbled to herself, "What have you done?"

CHAPTER
TWENTY

ESSIE made it to the station just in time to take the last bus to St. Louis. She had tried to use the bus ticket Jeanie had given after Andontis died, but the bus attendant told her it had expired. He also told her there weren't any buses scheduled to go to Chicago for three weeks and suggested she take the bus to St. Louis and then get a ticket from St. Louis to Chicago, and Essie did as he suggested. She had no way of contacting Jeanie to let her know she was coming—she didn't even know her address. She did remember the name of the place Jeanie had moved to and hoped that someone could show her how to get there.

As Essie settled into her seat and waited for the bus to pull away, she cried, thinking of her family. She felt guilty for leaving Naomi and Livi behind, and she cried over all the trauma she had experienced. She also cried because she had just murdered someone. Someone died by her hand, and she couldn't take it back, although she wished she could. She heard the bus doors close and felt the wheels begin to turn.

Essie stared out the window as the bus left the station. She watched the city in which she grew up become more distant, until she couldn't see it anymore. Thoughts of her family filled her mind. The family she had lost…and the family she had to lose in order to move on. She cried until she fell asleep. She was filled with sorrow each time she thought of Naomi and Livi. She loved them both so much, and she hated that she could no longer be a part of their lives. She kept telling herself she was doing this for them…but deep down, she was doing it to save herself.

Essie's dream

Essie was sitting in the field where she had just put out flames that were coming from the tree. She looked up and noticed her mother standing there with her back towards her. "Mama!" she cried. Sarah started to walk toward the tree that was standing in full bloom, and Essie chased her, trying to stop her. She felt like Sarah would be in danger if she touched it, but she couldn't catch up to her even though she was walking. "Don't touch the tree, Mama!" she called. Sarah didn't acknowledge her. She was almost to the tree when Essie caught her and grabbed her hand. Sarah turned to look at her, and she was crying.

Sarah looked down at her hands. She held a lantern in her left hand, and there was blood on her hand and on the lantern. There was a glass top on the lantern, and she removed it. Essie stood, watching her as she bent down and relit the tree with the fire from the lantern. Essie grabbed her hand and tried to stop her. Sarah took hold of her hand and wouldn't let go, even as she struggled. As the flames grew, Essie tried to pull away, but Sarah's grip was too strong. The fire started to burn Sarah from the bottom up. Essie noticed that she was holding Sarah's bloodied hand, and Sarah still wouldn't let go. Essie stopped struggling and watched as the fire burned Sarah's hand and then hers.

Essie woke up. She was back on the bus leaving New Orleans. She looked out the window and saw police lights, and she panicked. It looked like they were in the middle of nowhere. All she could see were dirt roads and police officers with their lights flashing and guns drawn. There were four police cars and an ambulance. Her fear increased, and she started to sweat. She looked for an escape route, but there weren't any. The police approached the bus, and Essie got up to go hide in the bathroom, but it was occupied. She turned back to her seat, and the officers got on the bus with their guns drawn. One of them had a picture in his hand. They went to every seat on the bus, checking the passengers. Essie pulled her hat down to cover her face, but the officers approached her seat and told her to remove it. She did so, knowing it was over. She was going to jail for murder.

The officer studied Essie then moved on to the next seat. She almost vomited into her hand. She was so scared. She let a sigh of relief; then took a napkin from her bag and wiped her face and hands. She had to take a minute to catch her breath. There was man sitting across from Essie. She didn't even realize he was there until he asked her if she was okay. It caught her off guard because she didn't think anyone was watching her. "Yes, I'm fine," she said. "Are you sure?" She nodded, and he said, "I could have sworn they were coming to get you." Essie stared at him for a minute, then rolled her eyes and sat back in her seat, waiting for the police to finish their business so she could get to Chicago.

A few minutes later, the police found who they were looking for. It was a couple who were together but riding in separate seats. The man was in the bathroom when the police got on the bus; and when they found him, they asked him about the woman he was with. She was in the front of the bus. The police had already checked her and moved past her, but he told them where she was. They handcuffed them both and took them to the police cars. "Wow. He is as dirty as they come." "Mmm...can't trust these men." They didn't even know she was there. He should've kept his mouth closed." Other women chimed in as the police left, and the bus pulled away, heading to St. Louis. Essie got out of her seat and walked to the front of the bus. As she got up, the man sitting next to her continued to watch her. "How much longer before we get to St. Louis?" she asked. "About an hour," the driver replied. She thanked him and returned to her seat.

About an hour later, the bus arrived in St. Louis, and Essie went to the window to buy a ticket to Chicago. As she approached, she saw the man that had been sitting across from her on the bus. She looked the other way and avoided eye contact, hoping that he wouldn't say anything to her. "Be careful out there, li'l lady," he said as he brushed past her.

It was almost four days before Essie finally arrived in Chicago. The ride from New Orleans to St. Louis seemed to have taken forever.

"Excuse me. Can you tell me how to get to the Standow Houses from here?" Essie asked a man who was standing out in front of the bus station, smoking a cigarette. "You mean the Standow Homes? You need to walk to State Street and catch the 29th Street bus. It will let you off right in front. Essie thanked him and walked away. She didn't know how to get to State Street, but he made her nervous, so she went back inside and asked at the ticket counter.

New Orleans: three months after Essie's departure

Naomi was awakened by someone banging on the front door. Livi didn't wake up. After Sarah's death and Essie's disappearance, Naomi wanted Livi to sleep with her because she didn't want to be alone. She left the bedroom and shut the door behind her. "Who's there?" she called softly through the door. "New Orleans Police Department," an officer said. She wondered what the police wanted with her and then she thought maybe they had found Essie and rushed to open the door. As soon as she unlocked the door, the police pushed the door open and rushed into the apartment, slamming her to the floor. One of the officers put his foot on her neck.

There were six officers. They had their flashlights on, and their guns drawn. "What's your name? Is anyone else here with you?" Naomi couldn't speak due to the pressure of the officer's foot on her neck. "I can't breathe," she muttered. Another officer pulled her up; and as she rubbed her neck and caught her breath, the officer asked again, "Is anyone here with you?" "Yes. My daughter Olivia is here. My name is Naomi Lavender." The officer asked for identification, and she pointed to her purse. Another officer reached in and pulled out her wallet. He looked at her, then looked at her ID.

"Do you know Ester Lavender?" "Essie is my sister," Naomi said. The officer asked where Essie was and when she had seen her last. She told him that she didn't know and that she hadn't seen Essie in three months. "Why are you asking about Essie? Have you found her?" Naomi asked. "Found her? So, you really don't know where your sister is?" "No, I don't. She just disappeared one day. She didn't give me any notice—she just didn't come home. I went to the police station after she didn't come home the first night, but they said I had to wait. When she didn't come home on the third day, I went back and filed a report. She hasn't called, and she didn't even leave a note.

Livi opened the bedroom door and started to walk toward Naomi. When she got to the end of the hallway, she tripped over one of her toys. One of the officers turned and aimed his flashlight at her. Livi started to cry and ran to Naomi. "My goodness, she is only three years old," Naomi said to the officer." "Here's my card, Ms. Lavender. If you hear from your sister, you need to call the station." "Why? Is she in trouble?" Naomi asked. "We need to ask her some questions. Questions about what?" Naomi replied. "I cannot say, ma'am. Just contact us if she comes back here."

Naomi walked back to her bedroom, put Livi down, and laid there wide awake. It was three o'clock in the morning, and she had to be up and out the door at six. After laying there for two hours, she got up and went to her closet, and pulled out the note that Essie had left.

Dear Naomi,

I know you are wondering why I am writing you this letter. I have to leave, and I won't be coming back. I hate that I have to do this because I love you and Livi so much, and I wish that I could stay. But I'm afraid if I do, I will put you both in danger, and I don't want that. I can't tell you where I'm going or why. Just know that I am safe. I will contact you as soon as I can but please do not try to find me. Do not worry or contact the police. I am okay. I love you with all my heart. Kiss Livi for me…and please don't let her forget me.

Love, Essie

Naomi found the note on Essie's bed after she'd gone to the police station the first time to file the report. "What did you do, Essie? What did you do?" Naomi whispered. She got her bottle of Canadian Reserve Whiskey out of the kitchen cabinet, poured a glass, and sat down at the kitchen table.

Epilogue

August 6, 2006

Walking into her office building in downtown Chicago with a medium hazelnut coffee from Dunkin' Donuts in one hand and her briefcase in the other, she smiled at the security officer. "Good morning, Artist," she said. "Good morning, Mrs. Franklin." "Hold the elevator," she called. She tried to run but couldn't because of the six-inch heels that she was wearing. Just as she got there, the elevator door started to close, and Artist put his hand out to hold it.

Mrs. Franklin looked backed at him and winked, then turned back and got on the elevator with all the White tenants and employees in the building. She smiled and said, "Good morning, everyone." No one said anything—she knew they wouldn't. She was one of the four Black women in the building who owned a company. "Excuse me," she said as she pressed the button to the 14th floor.

When she started her organization four years ago, she wanted to provide counseling services to Black women. Of course, she couldn't put that last part in her business plan; but ultimately, that was her goal. Plus, not many White women sought her services in the first place. She had only been leasing an office in the building on Madison and State Street for a little over a year. Her childhood dream was to work in one of the tall office buildings downtown; and because of the new city ordinances, she got that opportunity. The building she worked in was new, and they had to allow minorities the same opportunities as anyone else to lease space. In an office building that had thirty-nine floors, there were only twelve Black-owned companies: six on the 12th floor and six on the 14th floor.

"Good morning, Tonisha," Mrs. Franklin greeted her administrative assistant as she entered her office. "Good morning, Mrs. Franklin." She set her briefcase on the counter and asked, "What's on the schedule for today?" "Well, Tonisha started, "There's a young lady in your office." "In my office?" she asked. "Yes, but let me explain," Tonisha replied. "She was early for her appointment, but she was a mess when she came in. She's pregnant, and she couldn't stop crying. I didn't want her to interrupt anyone because she was really loud, so I let her go in there to wait for you." "Oh boy. Lord, right at the start of the day." She walked down the hall her office.

"Let me get this straight. You believe that your baby is in danger because of a curse on your family?" "Yes." "What makes you believe that there is a curse on your family?" The girl looked up, stared at the therapist with her bright blue eyes, and said, "My grandmother—her name is Essie…"

About the Author

TAWANA WILSON is the eldest of three children and grew up in a single-parent household on the south side of Chicago. She was literally born at home in her family's first floor apartment in the Robert Taylor Homes housing projects on Easter Sunday, March 26, 1978, due to a snowstorm that prevented the ambulance from getting through. Although these projects no longer exist, they were once infamous for their harsh living conditions and high criminal activity. Tawana became a mother at sixteen years old and was exposed to much trauma and turmoil.

After dropping out of high school and finding herself on public assistance, Tawana was required to take part in a program called Teen Parenting Services, where she was assigned an amazing case worker named Shirley Whitmore. Shirley helped her enroll at the Sullivan House Alternative High School and she graduated in 1997.

Tawana was determined not to have her son grow up as she had. In 2000, she enrolled in college and earned her first degree, an associate degree in Applied Science with a Major in Business Administration. She went on to earn a bachelor's degree in Business Administration with a Concentration in Management and a master's degree in Social Work.

In 2021, Tawana became a licensed social worker through the State of Illinois Department of Financial and Professional Regulations. She is currently the staff therapist for a non-profit organization in Chicago that is committed to reducing gun violence in the city's most at-risk neighborhoods. As the staff therapist, she provides clinical services that include intake and clinical assessments, individual and group therapy, and crisis intervention to young men participating in the organization's programs.

Tawana enjoys serving and giving back to the community. She is a faithful daughter of Christ and loves to share how the love of her Father has changed her and shaped her into someone that she could never have imagined becoming.

CONTACT THE AUTHOR

If you would like to contact the author, you may do so at:
Email: tawana5758@comcast.net